AN UNEXPECTED GIFT

MELANIE MORELAND

AN UNEXPECTED GIFT Melanie Moreland
Copyright © 2019 Moreland Books Inc.
Registration # 1164062
Ebook ISBN # 978-1-988610-28-3
Print book ISBN # 978-1-988610-27-6

MORELAND BOOKS INC.

Edited by

Lisa Hollett—Silently Correcting Your Grammar

Cover Art Adobe stock license
Photographer © Igor Link

INSTA-SPARK SERIES

When you want a bit of naughty along with the nice. Insta-Spark series from Melanie Moreland are complete standalone reads with one thing in common - lots of sweetness and a guaranteed HEA. Instant attraction, little angst - love and happiness abounds in this series.

#GetYourKissOn #ASprinkleofSugar #ASweeterRomance

DEDICATION

For Louise – my tea sister – thank you for
your friendship, and the many laughs.
This one is for you.

For friends and family,
my readers, and followers—
May love, peace, and joy surround you.
However you say it, however you celebrate—
May the wonder of the season fill you up.

And Matthew.
Always.
Love.

An unplanned journey
A change of direction
The meeting of two lost hearts

When Evan Brooks sets out to repair his fractured relationship
with his family, a broken-down car and an unplanned detour lead
him to Holly Cole.

Her eyes captivate him.
Her words comfort him.
Her heart warms him.

Is she the unexpected gift he's longed for?
Is this just a detour, or the road to happiness?
Find out in this heartwarming Christmas story.

EVAN

The night was black around me. With no streetlights or other cars to be seen, the inkiness seemed deeper—the snow falling on the cold winter night bright in the headlights. It was accumulating fast, the road becoming icy and slippery. I had to concentrate on driving, and my hands were tired from gripping the wheel.

The car lurched, made a strange noise, then sputtered and huffed, slowly rolling to a stop on the side of the road. I roared out in frustration.

"Goddammit!"

I leaned my head back on the headrest, trying to rein in my anger.

I knew the unpredictability of the Canadian winter. When the weather report says "chances of snow," it was a pretty damn certain thing.

What the hell possessed me to leave the quiet safety of my house to drive across the country two days before Christmas, to go see my family? What stupid sense of duty prompted my action?

I barked out a laugh, the sound loud in the car. So much for a surprise for them. The joke was really on me. They didn't know I was coming, and now, I wasn't sure I'd get there. From the strange sound my car had made just before it died, I wasn't sure I'd get home either. I was screwed either way.

I tried the engine again, but it wouldn't turn over. I slammed my hand on the steering wheel in exasperation.

I peered into the darkness, taking in the bleak landscape. I searched the back seat for the GPS I had flung over my shoulder in anger when the damn thing kept telling me to turn hard right and I almost ended up in a snowbank.

It lit up and came to life, the annoying voice repeating the same word over and again.

Recalculating.

I tossed it aside again—what a piece of junk.

I had no idea where I was, except I knew I was about three hours away from a major city. Ottawa was far behind me. My parents' home, some four hours or more ahead. I shook my head in frustration. I should have been patient and not taken that detour, but the accident on the highway had snarled traffic for miles. Instead of waiting for it to clear, I had followed a line of cars headed off the highway, but they had all disappeared right about the time my GPS died, followed not long after by my cell phone. I always forgot to charge the damn thing.

A car flew by me, and I lifted my head, narrowing my eyes as I watched it travel down the road. I pursed my lips as I saw brake lights and then they disappeared around a corner farther up the road. It was a long way away, but I was sure I saw lights.

What was up there?

A house? A business?

I shrugged my shoulders, knowing I had little choice in the matter.

There was only one way to find out.

I leaned over and grabbed my toque and gloves, silently cursing the fact that my leather coat wasn't going to offer much protection from the cold. Neither were my sneakers. But it was either go try to find a phone or sit in the car and wait for someone to stop. Given how little traffic there was right now, that didn't seem to be a viable option. I liked to run and could cover great distances in a short period of time, so I was sure I could make it to the location where I saw the light up ahead in short order.

Except, when I got out of the car, I realized there was a third option.

Freeze.

Damn, it was cold outside.

And thanks to the fresh snow, far too slippery to run.

With a low groan, I trudged down the road, my head bent against the wind and hands buried in my pockets, concentrating on staying upright. By the time I got to the spot I thought the other car had turned, my teeth were chattering, and my body shook with cold chills. Luckily the snow had let up, so I didn't have that to contend with as well. I rounded the corner and heaved a sigh of relief. Up ahead was a small building, its lights a dim glow. My pace quickened, and I pushed forward, groaning with relief when I realized it was a quaint little diner and it was open. The parking lot had about a half-dozen cars in it, and I gratefully pushed open the thick, wooden door and stepped through it.

The warmth inside the diner hit me, and I stumbled to the closest table, sitting down heavily with a low gasp. The air around me felt almost too hot compared to my icy skin. I pulled the toque from my head and yanked off my gloves, bending and stretching my cold hands, trying to get the feeling back in them. My glasses were so cold there was ice on the lenses, so I tugged them off and tossed them onto the table. I should have left them in the car. Since my laser surgery, I only needed them for reading, but I had left them on out of habit. I shut my eyes and breathed in the warm air in long gulps.

"Here." A low voice startled me.

I opened my eyes, meeting a pair of the lightest soft-blue eyes I had ever seen. They were filled with worry as they met mine, the emotion in them so clear. I couldn't remember the last time I had known anyone to look at me with such concern. It was an unusual feeling.

Unable to break our gaze, I blinked, and a deep V appeared between the lovely eyes.

"Can you talk?"

I cleared my throat and sat straighter. "S-sorry. Yes." My voice sounded rough, as if I hadn't spoken for days rather than only hours. "C-cold, I'm so cold."

A cup appeared in front of me on the table, and gratefully I grabbed for it, only to have it slip from my frozen hands and rattle back into place on the saucer.

I cursed and looked back up into the warm gaze. The woman attached to the lovely eyes smiled in understanding and lifted the cup to my mouth, helping me drink the warm liquid. She sat down, cupping the back of my head, the heat of her touch hot against my icy skin as I gulped down the coffee greedily. She set down the cup, a satisfied expression on her face when she saw it was empty.

"Better?"

I nodded, feeling the warmth seep through my body. "Much. Thank you."

"Where did you come from?"

"My car—" I paused and swallowed. "My car broke down."

Her voice was horrified. "You walked here from the highway?"

"No. The highway was closed. I followed some cars trying to get around an accident, and I got lost. My car started making some weird noises, and then it simply died. I walked for about twenty minutes."

"That's still a long way in this cold north wind. No wonder you're freezing. You don't even have boots on!" She tsked loudly as she stood. "Take off your coat. It's holding in the cold. Stay here."

She walked away, and I grinned at her retreating figure, finding her authoritative tone amusing for some reason. She was awfully little to be so bossy. I glanced out the window with a grimace, thinking about her command.

"Stay here."

Where did she think I was gonna go? Back out in that cold? That wasn't happening anytime soon.

She reappeared with a steaming bowl of soup and set it in front of me. Then she draped a blanket around my shoulders.

"Eat that. I'll be back."

Her tone brooked no argument. I picked up the spoon and took a mouthful. It was delicious, thick with vegetables, the steam welcome on my face. I ate it slowly, grateful for its warmth.

As I ate, I watched her move around the diner, talking to the customers sitting at tables, obviously at home here. She was short, five foot nothing, I guessed. Her strawberry-blond hair was chin length, curly and wild around her face. She was cute. Impish. Adorable, actually. She had a Christmas ornament tucked behind one ear, the sparkle on it catching the light, and it jingled as she moved her head. She was curvy and lush, her uniform snug over her full breasts, and she moved with an easy grace as she flitted from one task to the next. I had the feeling she was the sort of person who liked to stay active.

She smiled and laughed, filled coffee cups, sliced pie, and wiped off the tables as she teased customers. Her laugh brought a smile to my face. It was high and feminine—an odd sound to my ears that were used to the quiet and solitude. More than once, her gaze met mine, our eyes locking for a brief moment, before she returned to her task. It was as if she were checking up on me. I liked the odd feeling of her concern.

Feeling warmer, I glanced around, taking in my surroundings. It was an old-fashioned kind of diner, with Formica countertops and mismatched tables and chairs scattered around. A pass-through showed one cook, busy preparing food. The place smelled of burgers and grease, and there was a lingering sweetness in the air, no doubt from the pies and cakes displayed in a case on the counter. The sign taped to the glass boasted all desserts were made in-house.

Christmas lights were strung around the windows, and beside me, a rather dilapidated tree was festooned with popcorn strings and ornaments fashioned from straws and bent utensils, giving it a whimsical air that made me smile. The entire atmosphere was one of a well-worn, long-standing local place to gather and meet. At this time of night, the diner wasn't full, but the sign outside said it was open twenty-four hours. I wondered idly what time my bossy waitress worked until.

She reappeared, smiling in satisfaction at the empty bowl in front of me. "Warmer now?"

"Yes. Thank you again." I glanced at my watch, seeing it was after ten. "I don't suppose there's a twenty-four-hour service station around here?"

She shook her head. "No, sorry."

"A hotel close by?"

She frowned. "There is in town. A motel anyway."

I grimaced. "How far away is that?"

"About a twenty-minute drive."

"Ah."

"More coffee?"

"Will you help me drink it?" I teased, surprised at my words. I felt very at ease with this woman, which wasn't a normal reaction for me.

Her wide smile was beautiful. It transformed her soft, adorable features into a stunning vision of loveliness. A dimple appeared in one of her cheeks. Her eyes danced with mischief. She was heart-stopping. My breath caught in my throat looking at her.

"The first one is on the house. I charge after that." She tilted her head and winked. Her hair ornament tinkled with the movement.

"Noted." My voice dropped. "Thank you for your help. That was beyond kind."

Her cheeks flooded with color, enhancing her subtle beauty, and her gaze dropped. "I'll get your coffee."

On impulse, I held out my hand. "I'm Evan. Evan Brooks."

Her hand was warm, clasped in mine. "Holly Cole."

I looked down at our hands and then back up at her.

"Hello, Holly. It's a real pleasure to meet you."

A fresh cup of coffee appeared in front of me. I took a sip of it and gasped. "Wow. That's hot."

She smiled as she nodded. "I added cold water to the first cup so you could drink it fast and start warming up. Speaking of which, you're still shivering. Here." In her outstretched hand was a bundled towel. Confused, I took it from her grip only to realize it was warm.

"Your hands are still cold, so your feet must be freezing. They're soaking wet," she explained calmly. "Take off your shoes and you can wrap your feet in the towel."

"Oh, um…here?"

She nodded. "Yes."

I hesitated.

"Your feet," she said pointedly. "Take off your shoes and socks. The wet socks aren't helping."

I looked around the diner. I didn't want to get her into trouble. She smiled at me. "It's fine, Evan."

I toed out of my wet sneakers and socks and wrapped the towel around my feet. She was right—they were freezing. "Thank you," I said again. A shudder ran through me as the heat hit my skin.

"I called a friend in town who owns a garage. He's coming out with one of his tow trucks to get your car. They'll look at it in the morning. He can drive you to the motel as well. It's going to take him a while to get here, though, so I'll throw your socks and sneakers into the dryer in the back."

Again, I was surprised by her kindness. "Holly—thank you."

"It isn't a problem."

I reached for her, wrapping my hand around hers once more. There was a strange warmth when our skin connected. "You are truly —" I hesitated "—an angel. Thank you."

"Drink your coffee, Evan," she admonished.

But she was smiling as she walked away.

"You're sure?" Tom asked me as he pulled back into the diner parking lot, my car on the winch behind his truck. He'd picked me up and drove us to my car, but instead of riding back into town with him as planned, I felt the intense need to go back to the diner.

Back to Holly.

She had looked as sad as I felt when Tom arrived to take me to my car, even though she smiled as she handed me my now dry sneakers and socks. She wished me well and a safe journey before she turned away, leaving me feeling strangely empty. From the moment I left, I wanted to go back.

She had chatted with me while I waited for Tom, and I enjoyed her low voice and sweet laughter. My usual shyness seemed to disappear around her. I couldn't keep my eyes off her, following her movements as she busied herself with a seemingly endless list of tasks. I drank an inordinate amount of coffee and ate two slices of pie, just to get her over to my table. She had a way of drawing me into her warmth, making me want more.

More of her time and beautiful smiles. More of her.

I realized Tom was staring at me, waiting for my answer. "Yes. I left my glasses."

"I can wait."

"I'm, ah, hungry. I'll eat and then grab a cab."

Tom chuckled. "This isn't the big city, Evan. A cab will be hard to come by out here."

"I'll grab a ride with someone."

He glanced toward the diner. "The food *is* good." Then he smirked. "So is the service—or should I say, the staff—one in particular."

I narrowed my eyes at him. He returned my gaze steadily. "Holly is a good friend of my wife, Leslie, and me. We're both fond of her. Tread carefully."

"I just want a cheeseburger, Tom."

He laughed. "We have a Wendy's if that's all you're after."

"Um…"

"Carefully, Evan. Just saying." He paused. "I'll call your cell when I know what the problem is with your car."

Clutching my duffle bag and cell phone, I nodded as I got out of the cab of his truck.

"Thanks. Goodnight."

I watched him drive away, wondering what the hell I was doing. Then I headed back into the diner.

2

EVAN

A sweet smell hit me as I entered the diner, rich with cinnamon and sugar—it was obvious pies were being made for the next day. The scent was tantalizing. The diner was emptier than it had been earlier. I made my way to a table and sat down, placing my small bag on the chair beside me. Holly came out from the kitchen, her face breaking into a smile when she saw me. Once again, I was struck by how lovely she was as she walked toward me. She held up my glasses. "I was going to drop these off at the garage for you in the morning." Then she frowned as she glanced toward the window. "Why is Tom leaving? What is he doing? I told him you needed a ride to the motel!" She began to hurry toward the door before I stopped her.

"It's fine. I sent him back to town."

"Why? I'll get him back. You came for your glasses, and now you have them!"

I shook my head and drew in a deep breath. "I didn't come back only for my glasses. I wanted to spend more time with you."

Her light-blue eyes widened. "Oh."

I hesitated, worried about her reaction. "Is that okay?"

Pink tinged her cheeks. "Yeah, it is."

"Good."

"Can I get you something?"

I smiled. I hadn't totally lied to Tom—I was hungry. "May I have a cheeseburger? With fries?"

She laughed. "Yes."

"Will you-will you sit with me?"

"Yes."

"Okay. Good."

She nodded, suddenly looking shy. "Yes," she murmured. "Yes, it is."

"**D**on't you need to call your family?"

I shook my head. I finished chewing my burger and swallowed. I sipped my coffee, trying to figure out the best response. "They, ah, didn't know I was on my way."

"Oh, you're surprising them? I'm sure Tom will get your car fixed and you'll make it. They'll be thrilled."

I snorted. "I doubt *thrilled* is the right word."

She wrapped her hands around her mug of coffee, studying me over the rim. I noticed how small and delicate her fingers were, barely reaching around the mug.

"What would the right word be?"

"Surprised. Maybe slightly displeased."

Holly frowned. "That would be a strange reaction to have when family comes to visit at Christmas."

"They aren't—" I drew in some much-needed oxygen "—like most families."

She tilted her head as she processed my words. "Why would you say that?"

I sighed. "I don't get on well with my family, Holly." I chuckled dryly at the understatement. "When my car broke down, I was wondering if it was a sign I was stupid for making this trip."

"Why did you make it, then?"

I shrugged. "I haven't had a Christmas with them in years. My sister had a baby a couple of months ago. I thought maybe I should try to reconnect. Enough time had gone by, I thought perhaps I needed to make the effort."

Her tone was gentle. "What happened, Evan? Can you tell me?"

Her eyes were tender and kind. There were no demands in them, only concern. For the first time ever, I *wanted* to tell someone. I wanted to share. Unconsciously, I reached out my hand, and she met it halfway, wrapping mine between both of hers. Again, I felt a surge of warmth flow through me at the contact. I noticed the contrast between our skin. The tan on mine was still visible from all the work I did outdoors. My skin was rough and calloused. Holly's skin was pale, supple, and her hands looked small holding my larger one.

I glanced around. The diner was deserted except for a couple of truckers eating at the booth in the corner. They had already paid their bill and were finishing their coffee and pie. The cook was busy in the kitchen. No one was looking at us or paying attention to our discussion.

"I have two siblings. Both perfect in my parents' eyes. Popular in school, excellent at anything they put their mind to. Well-rounded students and now very successful adults. At least, their version of success. My sister is married, my brother an eternal bachelor. Both have great, high-profile careers." I smiled sadly, lifting one shoulder. "And then there's me. The baby of the family."

Holly smiled. "I thought the baby of the family was the most spoiled—the most loved."

I shook my head. "Not in my family. I've never quite measured up. I was always shy, quiet. I did well in school, but not like my siblings. I didn't participate in all the activities they did. My grades were good, and I liked to study and read. I liked to fix things and be on my own."

Memories pushed on the edges of my mind. My mother ordering me from the garage, telling me to stop working on a damaged table I had found and wanted to fix for my room.

"We do not have castoffs in this house." She grimaced in horror. *"Throw it back in the garbage where it belongs."*

She refused to listen to my pleas.

My father frowned at our exchange and muttered about my lack of ambition.

"Get your head out of your ass and concentrate, Evan. You'll never amount to anything at this rate. Brooks men don't use their hands like common laborers. We use our brains."

It never changed. I was constantly in trouble for wanting to fix and mend things I found and liked. Eventually, I stopped taking them home—instead using a friendly neighbor's garage, a man who liked to tinker and mend things as well. He taught me so many things I still used to this day. The day he died was one of the saddest days of my life. It felt as if I had lost my only friend, and I had no one to share my grief with. My family hadn't noticed how much time I spent with him. As long as I wasn't bothering them or doing anything to embarrass the Brooks name, they didn't really pay attention to me.

I shook my head to clear it, meeting Holly's eyes and returning to the present.

"I was never popular, good at sports, or outgoing the way they were. I was merely okay. Nothing exceptional like them. I was, as my father told me many times, an underachiever."

"Everyone is different. It's what makes us special."

I nodded because she was right. Except in my family—special wasn't allowed. It only made you different. Different wasn't good.

I studied our clasped hands, noting how well her fingers knit with mine. "My father is a lawyer. My brother, Calvin, is a partner in his firm. My sister, Kelsey, owns her own design company. My mother runs a high-end boutique. They all live in very large homes, drive expensive cars, and live extravagant lifestyles. They travel a lot, shop lavishly, and have lives I'm not comfortable with. I never was." I paused. "And then there's me. The odd man out." I barked out a low laugh. "The only thing I have in common with my siblings is our trust funds. And even those, we disagree on."

I stopped.

Why the hell had I mentioned my trust fund?

I never talked about it. Ever.

But Holly didn't comment on my trust fund. She didn't even look interested when I mentioned it.

"Tell me about Evan. Who is he?" she asked, squeezing my hand.

"I'm an antique restoration specialist. I live alone in a house on the edge of the water, in a little town on the East Coast. My world is a quiet one. My workshop is out back of my house, so I'm my own boss, and I don't socialize much. I live a simple, uncomplicated life. I don't live like my family. I like things…modest."

"Do you get lonely?"

I paused. I *had* been lonely until I took a job restoring an antique desk for Carol Whittaker. I hadn't realized how lonely I was until the Whittakers came into my life.

"Not the way I was when I was younger. I have a few good friends now who treat me like part of their family." I smiled as I thought about Dan and Carol. How they had practically adopted me, bringing me into their family, showing me what it was like to be *part* of one— accepted for who I was and not treated like an outsider. It took a lot of effort on their part to get me comfortable enough to accept their care and friendship since I wasn't used to being wanted. But they never gave up, and now I was no longer alone, although there were many times, I still felt lonely. Andrew, their son, and I were close friends, and I got along well with his wife, Tara, who treated me like the brother she'd never had, which meant she ordered me around a lot. Used to being ignored by my own siblings, I had to admit, I liked it.

"You repair broken pieces of history, Evan? Restore their beauty? Make them useful and vibrant again?"

I like how she phrased my work. "I suppose, in many cases, yes."

"I think that's wonderful. What else?" she prompted.

"I teach piano lessons in my spare time, and I like to carve things. I take a lot of pictures around the area I live in—it's beautiful there, no matter the season." I paused, searching my brain. "I like watching the history and nature channels. And I coach little kids' hockey in the winter."

She lifted our hands and studied mine. "You have long fingers— perfect for the piano."

I chuckled. "I never get them clean, though. No matter how I scrub them, there's always stain or paint under the nails from whatever project I'm working on."

She smiled and shook her head. "They're still beautiful hands, Evan. Capable, strong, talented hands."

I looked down at them in surprise. She thought they were beautiful? Capable and talented?

I was certain no one had ever used those words to describe any part of me.

I looked at her hands: small, tiny fingers that barely came to my knuckles as I held them against mine. I liked, however, how they felt nestled between my own fingers. They seemed to fit as if they belonged there.

"What about you?" I asked. "What do you like to do?"

"I rescue stranded men. Like a St. Bernard—except I have less fur. And no brandy."

I chuckled. "Happens a lot, does it? Strange men tripping in here half frozen, looking for warmth?"

She nodded. "A regular Wednesday night occurrence." She winked. "At least once a month."

I laughed at her drollness. "What do you do aside from imitating a big, furry dog?"

She paused, her hesitation making it seem as if she weren't sure how to answer. I wondered if perhaps no one ever asked her that question.

"I-I like to sketch. Paint with watercolors." She shrugged. "I'm not very good, but I like doing it."

"You're probably amazing."

"Why would you say that?"

It was my turn to shrug. "No idea—a feeling, I suppose. I think you'd be amazing at anything you did."

Her gaze skittered away and I knew I was right. No one asked, and she never talked about it. It was something private. But she had told me.

14

"What do you sketch?"

"I take walks and sketch animals in the woods. Sometimes the sunsets. I just enjoy it."

"You'd love it where I live. There is so much beauty, you'd be sketching all the time."

She offered me a small smile, her gaze unfocused as she looked past my shoulder into the night. I wasn't sure why I'd said that, but for some reason, I wanted her to know about the beauty of the place I called home.

"Do you have, um, a girlfriend?" she asked, looking at me bashfully from under her eyelashes. Then as if she realized what the answer to that question might be, she started to withdraw her hands from mine.

"No," I hastened to assure her, holding on to her fingers. "I'm, ah, not so good with...girls. Um, women. I mean, I've had them. Girl-friends, I mean. A few. But, yeah, um. No. No girlfriend." I huffed out a sigh. "The shyness I suffered from in my youth has never completely gone away. I have trouble talking at times."

God, I was lame.

"Seems to me you do okay. You're talking to me."

"You're different, somehow," I murmured. "You make it easy to talk to you."

The blush I found so charming appeared again. "Thank you."

I squeezed her hand.

"Tell me more about your home," she asked.

"I live in a log cabin. A family had bought it as a holiday place, then grew tired of it. I saw it one day when I was traveling and fell in love with it. I bought it and spent a year adding on to it, building my work-shop and making it my own."

"You were traveling?"

I stared out the window, lost in thought. "I knew my life was never going to satisfy my parents. After I left school, I knew I didn't want a nine-to-five job. I had secretly been taking woodworking courses, and I knew that was what I wanted to do. I left home and traveled, learning more and more about antiques and restoration. I was in

Nova Scotia when I saw the house." I shrugged. "Walking up the driveway felt like coming home to me, and I stayed."

"That's amazing."

"My favorite time of day is spent sitting on my porch watching the sun set over the water," I offered quietly. "It's so peaceful. I love living there."

"Sounds pretty good to me."

I snorted. "According to my father, it's a waste."

She lifted one shoulder dismissively. "It's not his life. He lives his life how he likes. You're entitled to live yours. You don't owe them anything. You only owe your life to yourself."

Her words hit me.

Unassuming. Direct.

My life.

Not his.

I stared at her in shock at the simple clarity of her statement.

"Still, they are your family, Evan. You should try to be part of their life. Family is important."

"Do you have family, Holly?"

Her glance was unfocused over my shoulder. The diner was now empty except for us, the only other sound in the place coming from the kitchen. It was well after two, and she had told me that she worked until three. I didn't want the time to be over.

I waited as she gathered her thoughts.

"I lost my parents a couple of years ago. They were away on one of their trips and died when the bus they were on crashed in the mountains of Brazil. I have no siblings. So, no family—I'm alone." She stopped as if searching for words.

"One of their trips?" I prompted.

"My parents were free spirits. We relocated a lot, never settling—always moving from some new adventure they wanted to have to another. They worked so many odd jobs, never saving for the future, and when they died, there was nothing left for me. I hadn't gone on that trip with them. I hadn't gone for a couple of years. I was tired of the travel, to be honest. After they were gone, I stayed here. I was tired

16

of moving around, being dragged from place to place. I had a job and a few friends. I needed to stay in one place for a while and figure out what I wanted to accomplish in my life."

I frowned. It didn't sound like she'd had a very good childhood.

"Is that why you like to sketch?"

She nodded. "A pad of paper and a pencil were easy to carry around. I could lose myself in the view—commit some place I liked to memory." She sighed. "We never stayed anywhere for very long, and I knew we'd probably never go back. My parents believed in experiencing something—someplace, once—and going forward." There was a beat of silence. "I often think I was one of those things."

"Sounds lonesome."

She met my gaze. "It was."

"How old are you, Holly?"

"Twenty-three."

"I'm thirty."

"It's just a number, Evan."

"True. Do you, ah, do you live alone?"

"With my cat, Chester. I have a roommate who is hardly ever there. Connie travels for a living and comes home every so often to swap her wardrobe, catch up, and she's gone. It's her place—I sort of take care of it while she's gone."

"You like it here?"

She shrugged. "I was so tired of never having anything to call my own—never feeling I truly had a *home*. I wanted someplace I felt I could belong."

"Did you find it?"

Her voice was so low, I almost didn't hear her. "Not yet."

The urge to lean forward and tell her I wanted to help her with that was strong. Instead, I squeezed her hands. "We all want that, Holly. We all need to belong—to someone and someplace."

She nodded.

"What do you want from your life?"

"I want to go back to school and get my degree. I want to work with kids. I love kids."

"You want to teach?"

"Teach or early childhood development. I'm still deciding."

"Is that—" I paused, unsure how to ask "—going to happen for you?"

"Soon." She nodded. "I work here and part time in town at the local grocery store. I'll have enough to go to school in the fall next year. I'll still have to work and find a place to live with roommates, but I'll be able to do it."

"That's great." I squeezed her hands in encouragement. I had a feeling she could do anything she put her mind to.

The door opened, and an older woman walked in. She stared briefly at Holly and me before nodding and heading into the back. It was then I realized how close we were. Our chairs were pulled together, shoulders touching. Our hands were entwined on the table-top, and as we talked, our heads had drifted nearer together, almost touching. It was as if we were wrapped in a bubble of our own, sharing our lives with each other. I had never experienced this sense of intimacy with another person...or this sense of wanting to be even closer.

"My shift relief is here," she told me. "That's Barb."

"Does she work every night?" I couldn't imagine getting up in the middle of the night all the time.

Holly grinned mischievously and bent forward, her voice discreet. "Yes. Rumor has it she likes how Ronnie, um, *runs the kitchen—*" she winked "—if you know what I mean. Worth getting out of bed for, I hear." Then she giggled, and I chuckled with her.

"What about you, Holly? Do you like his kitchen *skills?*" I teased her, even though inside I was feeling a strange tightening of my stomach as I waited for her answer.

She relaxed back in her chair. "Nope. He's always too hot—working by the stove." She quirked her eyebrows, making her look adorable. "I prefer cold hands and feet. Gives me something to warm up while cuddling."

I laughed at her cheeky remarks. She *was* quite adorable.

She yawned—trying to cover the fact that she was doing so by turning her head.

My smile faded, because I knew what that meant. It was time to say goodbye to her. I stood.

"You must be tired, and it's time for you to go home. I need to find a ride into town."

She reached out her hand, grabbing mine, and pulling me back into my chair. "I'll take you."

"You don't have to—" I hesitated, but I really wanted a little more time with her.

"Don't be silly. I'm going into town anyway."

"Yeah?"

She nodded. "I, ah, just have to do a few things."

I released her hand regretfully. "Take your time." I grinned, pleased at the offer. "I'm not going anywhere."

She disappeared into the kitchen, my eyes following her movements, my head echoing with one small phrase I couldn't understand.

"*Not without you.*"

"This is what you drive?" I gaped at the monster truck sitting in the last spot in the parking lot. "Can you see over the dashboard?"

Holly chuckled. "Yes. It was the one thing that came with us, everywhere we went. And one of the few things I have left of my parents. It's an old friend."

"Is it safe?" Old friend or not, it looked like it had seen better days.

She snorted. "Get in, fraidy cat."

I climbed in, and a few seconds later, Holly had the engine cranked up and the heater going. "It just takes a few minutes to warm up."

"Okay."

Our eyes met and held in the dim light coming from the dashboard. The cab got warm. Very warm. I swallowed nervously. Holly's bright eyes reflected the light as she stared at me, her gaze unsure.

Slowly, I lifted my hand, grazing my fingers over her cheek. "You've been so kind to me all night, Holly. More than you know."

"I just helped you warm up," she whispered, searching my eyes with her own.

"Yes, you did that. But you talked to me and listened. You *cared* for me. That is so...*special*. I can't thank you enough."

"You're welcome."

Bravely, I slid closer, reaching over to stroke her round cheek again. "You truly are an angel to me."

"I've never been an angel to anyone."

I drew in a long breath, my fingers slipping into her hair. "Well, you're mine. My Angel."

Her eyes widened.

And then my mouth was on hers.

Warm, sweet, indulgent.

She wound her arms around my neck, clutching the back of my hair with tender fingers. When I slipped my tongue inside her mouth, the sound she made was erotic. I pulled her closer, my tongue stroking hers. I cupped the back of her head, holding her close. I never wanted to stop kissing her. It was only the bright lights of a car pulling in and reflecting in the rearview mirror that had us pulling apart, panting. My finger traced her bottom lip. "Should I apologize?"

"No."

"Can I do that again?"

"Yes," she breathed.

"Thank God," I whispered against her lips.

I had no idea how long I kissed her. I didn't know how I even got brave enough to kiss her in the first place, but now that I had, I didn't want to stop. Finally, though, she broke away, her breath warm on my cheek as she snuggled her head into my shoulder. I held her against me, enjoying the closeness.

"Evan?" Her voice was muffled against my chest.

I kissed her head. I liked how my name sounded on her lips. "Hmm?"

"Will you...will you come home with me?"

I tilted up her chin and studied her open gaze. No one had ever looked at me with so much emotion before. It was overwhelming. "*God,* Holly, I want to. I want to so much. Are you sure?"

"Yes."

I drew in a deep breath and kissed her again. "Take me there, then."

3

EVAN

The house she lived in was small. There was the glow of a tiny light coming from the inside. I could see the silhouette of Holly's cat in the window, no doubt waiting for her to come home. Holly shut off the engine, and for a moment the truck cab was silent.

I swallowed hard, thinking she had changed her mind. We had been quiet the whole drive, but our hands were entwined on the seat between us. I stroked her silky skin with my thumb, occasionally lifting her hand to brush my lips over it, when the urge to do so became too strong to resist. Now, I tightened my grip. "I can walk to the motel from here, Holly. It's okay."

Her gaze flew to mine. "No! I...I just need you to know I don't do this. I don't bring men home with me."

"I don't do this either," I admitted. "It's been a long time for me, and I don't have what you might call a great deal of experience with women."

This time, she squeezed my hand. "I don't have a great deal of experience either."

Her honest words made me ridiculously happy.

"I, ah, wasn't really planning on, um," I stammered. "I don't have—" My voice trailed off in embarrassment.

Holly chuckled. "Connie keeps a stock of condoms on hand. I'm sure she won't mind if we borrow a few...or, um, more if needed."

More?

My smile couldn't be contained. Holly's answering smile was shy but heartwarming.

"I feel something between us. Something I've never felt before with you. Can you feel it?" I asked.

"Yes."

"Are you sure about this, Holly?"

She drew in a deep breath and opened her door. "Yes."

S he led me into the dark house, flicking on another small lamp in the living room. I was surprised not to see any Christmas decorations or a tree. She was such a warm person—somehow, she seemed the type to surround herself with the season. Even I dragged home a small tree each year from the woods behind my house, and although my decorations left a lot to be desired, it was a nice thing to look at in the dark evenings when I was alone. I looked at her curiously. "No tree?"

She shrugged. "I work tomorrow, and then on Christmas Day, I'll have dinner with Leslie and Tom later in the day. I don't exchange gifts with anyone anymore." She laughed, the sound more sad than happy. "Not that I ever really did. My parents never made a big deal about Christmas. They felt it was too commercial, so they didn't do very much. Occasionally, there was a small gift by my plate in the morning."

"Occasionally?"

"Sometimes, there was nothing. It depended on if they were working, how long we'd been living in the place we were in, that sort of thing." She paused. "Maybe one day, it will be different. But for now, it seems silly to do anything only for me."

I swallowed around the painful lump in my throat. For the first time since I met her, she sounded despondent. Resigned. Whereas

Christmas for me growing up had been excessive in the worst form, with too many gifts simply for the sake of giving gifts, hers had been the exact opposite. It also sounded to me as if she was as ignored as I had been as a child. I hated that she knew that feeling. I also hated the fact that she didn't feel she was worth the effort to add some holiday joy into her life.

What was it about this woman that made me want to give her every single desire she ever had missed out on? I wanted to fill her small house with lights and tinsel and put a tree in the corner that was loaded with gifts. I wanted to watch her open them and see the delight on her face. I wanted to be the one who made her smile. I wanted to share in her joy. I blinked at the peculiar feeling; it was another emotion I had never experienced before.

A strange noise had me looking down to see a pair of green eyes gazing up at me. Long dark fur stuck out everywhere and a patch of white was centered on his forehead. Bending down, I stroked the softness. "You must be Chester." I was rewarded with a deep purr as the cat wound itself around my legs, then stretched up, allowing me to pick him up. Holly giggled, the sound so much better than her earlier, sadder sound.

"He must like you. He never lets people pick him up."

"Have you had him long?"

"No. I found him last winter outside the diner. I think someone had abandoned him. I brought him home to keep him safe for the night, but I couldn't bear the thought of taking him to a shelter. So, he stayed."

I smiled at her. Of course, he did. Her rescuing me tonight wasn't a first for her. I wondered if maybe she would let me stay as well. The strange thought made me pause for a moment.

"He's so small."

She nodded, reaching over to scratch his head. "I think he had a hard life before I found him. He never grew very much." Then she giggled again. "He looks like you."

"What?" I chuckled.

"The green eyes and the white patch on his head. There is quite the resemblance."

I grinned. I had developed a white streak at the front of my hairline when I was young. My mother disliked it and had insisted on having it colored, but I stopped doing that as soon as I left home. "Your taste in strays is excellent."

"I only save the handsomest men."

I blinked at her. *Handsome?* She thought I was handsome?

"I'm a throwback," I blurted out.

"What?"

"I heard my mother tell someone once I was a throwback to my grandfather, whom my father didn't get on with. I looked exactly like him—right down to the white patch in my hair. I have his coloring and eyes too. She said it was probably why my father wasn't very fond of me."

Her eyes were wide. "Your mother said your own father wasn't *fond* of you?"

I shrugged. "It wasn't much of a secret."

"That is so...cold."

"I was never treated the same way as the other two." I paused. "I don't think any of them found me very handsome. I looked different, I wore glasses. The way I saw things, *did* things, was different." I laughed mirthlessly. "My entire family is opinionated, vocal. Far too much, in my opinion. I was always in the corner and quiet. I never fit in."

"You're a gentle soul."

"My father would say weak."

"Forgive me for saying this, Evan, but your father is an ass."

I couldn't help but laugh. She was so right about that.

Her voice became quiet. "They were wrong. About everything. You're wonderful—just the way you are."

"You think so? How can you be so sure?"

She shrugged. "I'm a good judge of character."

I set down the cat and stepped closer. "And you like my character, Holly? You think I'm handsome?"

She reached up and ran her fingers through my hair. "Yes. I like you. And yes, I think you're very handsome."

"All my family had light-colored hair and hazel eyes, like my parents. I have my grandfather's dark hair and green eyes, plus his white streak. Even physically, I was the odd one."

"You're not odd. You're Evan. You're perfect."

Her words were like a small shock running through my system.

Nobody had ever thought or told me I was perfect. I couldn't describe the feelings those words elicited.

I leaned into her touch as she continued to stroke my hair. The sensation was wonderful. No wonder the cat purred. If I could, I would as well.

"I'm not perfect. I'm far from it."

"Not as far as you've been led to believe. You look sad, the same way Chester did when I found him."

"I've been lost all my life," I whispered.

"So have I."

Her hand stilled. The air around us warmed again. Our eyes held, locked in a silent conversation.

Holly swallowed. "Do you want a drink, Evan?"

I shook my head.

"Something to eat?"

"No."

I pulled her closer.

"There is only one thing I want right now."

Her voice was hushed, almost shy. "What is it?"

"I want you, Angel."

And then her mouth was on mine.

I wasn't lost anymore.

There was no shyness between us. It felt as though I had known her forever. As though in some other life, we had experienced each other on this intimate level. It was as if I had found a missing part of me.

Holly's hands were so gentle; they touched me with such tenderness, I wanted to weep. The way she stroked my torso, played with my nipples, touched my face. Her mouth was talented and warm, her lips an artist's brush that painted my body like a canvas with bold strokes and delicate arches. I groaned and hissed my pleasure as she explored me.

Nothing was rushed or hurried. There was no screaming or wild thrashing. There was only a deep, abiding passion between us I had never experienced with anyone else.

Slowly, sensually, we shed our clothes, kissing and touching as each new piece of skin was uncovered. Our voices murmured and encouraged, whispering adoration and sweet promises. I caressed her curves, loving how she felt under my touch—supple and perfect. Her skin was warm, silky, and tasted sweet under my tongue. I discovered all her secrets, her ticklish right side I teased mercilessly, the small scar on her thigh I kissed tenderly. I learned the dip of her waist. The rightness of her rounded hips. The beautiful fullness of her breasts. I thrilled at how she whimpered as I kissed the juncture at the base of her neck, teasing it with my tongue. Moaned when I sucked on her nipples.

Our mouths locked together, our bodies in flawless sync. Being buried inside her was nothing short of perfection. Her warmth grounded me, her sighs filled my head, and feeling her coming around my cock, as I moved and rocked above her, was ecstasy in itself. She held me close as I stilled, a low, heavy groan escaping my throat, my own orgasm so powerful, there was only one word I was able to utter, the most important one in the world at the moment.

Angel.

Wrapped up in her arms afterward was like coming home. She was so right curled around me. I had never experienced contentment before or this odd feeling of happiness. Both were foreign and both were abundant, coursing through my body and leaving me filled with wonder at all the emotions she seemed to bring out in me.

I looked down at Holly, the source of those strange feelings. Her cheeks were flushed in the dim light, her eyelashes resting on them as she relaxed against me. I could feel her stuttering breaths against my neck as her body softened. I knew my breathing was still erratic. Slowly, we relaxed and calmed, still wrapped around each other. I nuzzled the top of her head, smiling as she tilted back her head, looking shy as she gazed up at me.

"Hi."

I kissed her full mouth. "Hi," I whispered against her lips.

"That was—" She bit her lip. "Wow." She grinned.

Now it was my turn to feel shy. I knew I wasn't the most experienced lover. It had certainly been the most intense experience I'd ever had. "Yeah? It was, ah, *good* for you?"

She pursed her lips. "Well, now that you mention it—"

"Um," I stammered.

She pressed closer, flinging her leg over my hip and cupping my ass. "Maybe we should try again, just to be sure?"

A slow grin broke out on my face. "To be sure of...?"

"That it was as beautiful as I think it was."

My heart soared. I rolled, hovering over her, already hardening and wanting her. "Yes. We need to make sure of that."

4

EVAN

My cell phone rang from Holly's bedside table the next morning. She'd plugged it in for me the night before so Tom could reach me. I blinked in the bright morning light. We'd been up most of the brief night, only dozing, talking, and sharing long, lingering kisses. We'd made love again, and even now as I watched her lean over to grab the phone, I could feel myself stirring with desire for her. She handed me the phone, and I cupped her head, bringing her close for another kiss before answering it.

Tom's booming voice told me he found the problem and, luckily, was able to get the parts he needed. My car would be ready by noon. I thanked him and hung up, feeling an odd pull in my chest. I should be grateful I could get back on the road today, yet I felt only sadness that I would be able to leave in a few hours.

Holly kissed me, her voice quiet. "What time?"

"Noon."

"I can drop you there before I go to work."

"What time do you work until?"

"Only six today. The diner closes early since it's Christmas Eve."

"Holly—" I wanted to say something. What, I had no idea, but something.

She shook her head, her voice beseeching. "Don't."

My head fell back on the pillow, my eyes shutting against the burn I felt behind them. I pulled her close, breathing in the scent of her hair. She smelled like sun and flowers. Lovely. "I have so much to say."

"This was a stop in your life, Evan. A detour. Maybe one you needed, to be able to *find* your life. But you have to keep going. I don't expect anything." Her voice lowered. "Last night was so wonderful. I'll treasure it and the thought of you always. I'm glad you found my diner."

I swallowed. I was more than glad I'd found her diner. And her. She was an unexpected gift in my life. Perhaps the greatest I would ever receive.

"Tell me about your life, your friends," she whispered. "Don't tell me goodbye yet."

I tightened my hold and did what she asked. I told her about Dan and Carol. Andrew and Tara. How they had drawn me into their world, showing me a real family was like. Loving. Caring. Supportive. Not judgmental and cold.

"I'm glad you found them."

I chuckled. "Carol found me, actually. And she refused to let me stay in my shell. It was as if she saw what I needed and was determined to give it to me, whether I knew I wanted it or not."

I described my house as best I could, telling her about the renovations I had made and the huge porch I had added on to the front.

"The sunsets, Holly. They're breathtaking and remind me every day how much I love living there. I make a point of sitting on the porch and watching them. I feel a sense of peace."

"It sounds beautiful. Maybe one day, I'll go there."

I had to bite my lip to stop myself from telling her I wanted her to come and be with me there—that I wanted her to see the sunsets with me every day. I knew it was only the emotion of this trip causing me to feel that way. Instead, I hummed. "You could sketch and paint something new every day."

I made her chuckle with some stories of restoration disasters— glued hair and throbbing thumbs from miscalculated blows of my tools. She told me funny stories of the diner and of growing up, as she put it, like a gypsy.

Throughout it all, we touched. She swept her fingers over my skin, warming it as they went. I kept her close, my hand often buried in her wild hair to tilt her head back for a kiss. Chester slumbered away at the bottom of the bed, frequently stretching, pushing on my feet as he made himself more comfortable.

The room became still. Finally, she asked, "How much longer to your parents' place?"

"About four hours."

"So you'll get there late afternoon."

"I have to stop somewhere and pick up some gifts. This was such a last-minute decision, I didn't bring anything with me." I shuddered, thinking about entering a mall on Christmas Eve. I wasn't big on crowds.

She sat up, tugging the blanket with her to cover her beautiful breasts. "Evan, there's a lovely gift shop here. Local artisans. Tom's wife, Leslie, runs it. She doesn't open until noon, but I know she would let me bring you in early, if you'd like. You could pick out some things, she would wrap them for you, and you could drive straight through." She paused. "Then I wouldn't worry."

"Worry?"

"It gets dark early. I'd like to know you got to your parents' before it got dark, especially today. I'll worry because of your car." She smiled even though I could see the deep sadness in her eyes. "I'm not sure there'll be another diner for you to find open tonight."

My breath caught. She was concerned about me again. She cared. I drew my fingers over her cheek and pulled her back down to me. She buried her face into my neck.

"There will never be another diner—or another you, Angel."

Her voice almost broke me. "Make love to me, one more time?"

How could I say no?

31

Hours later, I held out my credit card for the purchases. All picked out with the help of Holly, all tasteful, thoughtful gifts most people would be thrilled to receive. Handmade silk scarves for my mother and sister, carved business card holders for my brother and father, beautifully knitted items for my new niece, along with a handmade teddy bear with arms and legs that moved. There was even a hand-painted silk tie for my brother-in-law. I knew, though, my family would be unimpressed by the choices. No brand names, expensive trinkets, or extravagant gestures were in the gifts. None of them would be deemed acceptable. But I didn't say a word. I appreciated Holly's assistance and enthusiasm. I knew she thought the gifts would be accepted and enjoyed. I refused to tell her otherwise—she had been so delighted and wanted to help; I couldn't bear to disappoint her. The gifts would find homes elsewhere, but not with my family. Of that, I had no doubt.

The gifts Holly helped me pick for the Whittaker family would, I knew, be treasured and loved simply because they came from me. Those gifts, I found joy in purchasing. Holly had great taste, and surprisingly, the shop was filled with a vast assortment of beautiful and useful items. I saw the way Holly's eyes lit up at some of the items she looked at, and I had to resist the urge to buy them all for her. She would hate that. This was something she wanted to do for me, and she didn't want it to be about her at all.

I accepted the bags of wrapped gifts, Holly having asked Leslie to keep the two groups separate, and we walked to the truck, my heart growing heavier with each step.

We were silent on the drive back to her house, and I followed her inside, my stomach clenching and throat going dry at the thought of what would happen next.

She had to go to work, and I had to finish my drive and go see my family. Our time was done. The unexpected gift of her sweet, caring nature was about to end. After Tom had called, we'd made love, showered in her small bathroom, and shared some more time in her kitchen, sipping coffee, neither of us hungry for food. My car had been picked up and was now beside hers outside, ready to go.

For a moment, we stood in her tiny kitchen, staring at each other, and then she was in my arms. I lifted her up, holding her tight.

"My Angel," I whispered against her ear. "What you've given me these past hours—I can't even begin to say thank you."

Her arms tightened. "You are so much more than you give yourself credit for, Evan. You have such a beautiful soul. Don't let them take that away from you." Her lips touched mine in a gentle caress. "Live your life for you. Find what makes you happy and grab it. Act on that happiness."

She began to step back, but I held on. I couldn't let her go—not yet. The words were out of my mouth before I realized. "I need more time."

"What?"

"I need more time with you."

"But your family—"

"Will be there tomorrow. They don't even know I'm coming, so it doesn't matter if I show up today or tomorrow. You told me to act on what makes me happy. You make me happy."

"I have to go to work."

"That's fine. I'll be here when you get home. Spend the evening with me. Let me wake up with you tomorrow morning. *Christmas morning.* I want to wake up with someone who cares about me." I paused. "Whom I care about. I want to wake up with you."

She stared at me, her eyes wide with anxiety and longing. They reflected the same emotions I was feeling.

"Please give me this, Holly. A few more hours is all I'm asking."

"Yes," she murmured. "I want you to stay."

I pulled her close, feeling as if I could breathe again. I knew I was only delaying the inevitable, but for now, I could stay and be with her. Tomorrow was hours away.

Today, I had her.

5

EVAN

"I 'll drive you to work," I offered, my arms still looped around her waist. I felt as if a weight had been lifted from my shoulders. As if I had given myself a gift today—a gift of *her*.

"Oh, um, I have a couple errands to run. The diner won't be busy, so Judy and I cover for each other for an hour, then we can get things done—so I'll need my truck."

I glanced out the window at her mammoth vehicle in the driveway. In the light, I could see how old and decrepit it was. I had thought it a dull red in the dark last night, but today I could see the rust on the body was what was holding it together, covering the gray the truck used to be. But she insisted it was roadworthy, and I had no choice but to accept it.

"All right," I agreed. "But before you go, I need to know where a couple of places are in town."

Holly laughed, her eyes no longer sad. "What are you going to do while I'm gone?"

I grinned, feeling lighter than I had since I woke up. I had more time with her.

"I've got some stuff to do. Then Chester and I will hang out."

She narrowed her eyes, looking suspicious. "*Stuff*? What are you up to, Evan Brooks?"

I liked how my name sounded rolling off her tongue, the bossiness of her tone as she settled one hand on her hip and acted stern. She was too cute.

"I'm going to cook you dinner."

"You cook?"

I snorted. "I live by myself in a small town. There's no fast food close. It was either learn to cook or starve. I do pretty well." I winked at her. "You do like tacos, right?"

"Um, sure."

Laughing, I pulled her back into my arms. "I can do a little better than that. I'll follow you, and you can point out where the grocery store is."

"And you'll be here when I get back?"

I kissed her, liking the thought of being here, waiting for her. "Yes."

She sighed, the sound happy and content. She lifted up on her toes and kissed me in return. "Okay."

I followed Holly all the way to the diner, some odd sense of needing to make sure she was okay filling my head. She hopped out of her truck and approached my car, bending low into the window.

"Not necessary, Evan. The truck looks awful, but Tom keeps it running well."

"Maybe I just like following you. You have an awesome tailgate."

She blinked, then started to giggle. I grinned at her amusement, loving the fact that it was me who made her smile. She leaned in and kissed me, her tongue gliding along my bottom lip. I slid my hand up her neck and kissed her back, groaning low in my throat, desire for her building fast. She pulled back, her cheeks flushed.

"Wow, you can kiss."

I tugged on her neck. "Come back, and I'll show you some more."

She laughed and stepped away from the car. She touched her mouth, shaking her head. "Later, Evan."

I watched her walk away, leaning out my window, unable to help myself.

"Yep," I called. "*Awesome* tailgate."

Her laughter drifted across the parking lot. She paused at the door, peering over her shoulder. She blew me a kiss I pretended to catch, then she disappeared. I grinned all the way back into town.

I pulled back into the parking lot at Leslie's store, not surprised to find it busy. She looked at me oddly when I walked in, then approached me once she was finished with her customer.

"Changed your mind about one of your gifts, Evan?"

I ran my hand along the back of my neck. "Ah, no. Change of plans. I need a few more presents." I paused. "For Holly."

A smile lit her face. "That, I can help you with."

I returned her smile. "I was hoping you'd say that." I sucked in a deep breath. "I want to spoil her a little."

"Then let's go shopping."

Hours later, I looked around, making sure everything was in place. A small tree was set up in the corner, the white lights and pretty ornaments I had bought shining in the dark. Some bright parcels were nestled underneath. I had even remembered a small gift for Chester. Earlier, I had resisted the urge to buy everything I had seen Holly's eyes linger on when we'd been shopping together for my family's gifts, but I did get some things I knew she would like. Special ones, just like her. Leslie helped guide me to choose the perfect ones, although one I had chosen alone. But from the way Leslie's eyes had lit up, I knew I had chosen well. She had her assistant wrap them all, so they were festive and pretty under the tree.

I resisted adding any other decorations to Holly's place, but I did get some flowers for her and added some scented candles I had seen at Leslie's. As I was setting things up, I realized how sparse the house was of regular decor. Her roommate, Connie, kept the place only for a home base, but it made me unhappy to think that Holly was so used to having nothing static in her life, she simply didn't think to make where she was living into a home for herself. She had never known that, and she didn't think herself worthy of the effort.

While I was out, I had picked up a couple of Christmas movies to watch and some snacks when I was at the small grocery store. The thought of spending the evening on the sofa with Holly curled up beside me made me absurdly happy. I wanted the night to be a good one for both of us. Two lonely people enjoying spending some time together at a time of year when being alone seemed so much darker than usual. I ignored the small part of my brain telling me it wasn't going to be possible to be alone again after today. That I wasn't going to be able to walk away from Holly. I liked how I felt when I was with her; she banished the sadness that seemed to hover over everything I did.

I shook my head to stop those thoughts. I only had until tomorrow with her.

I checked the dinner in the oven and made sure the wine was getting cold. I hoped she would enjoy the meal I'd made for us. I wasn't a gourmet cook and the stuffing was from a package, but my roast chicken was usually pretty stellar. I did hope Holly could make gravy, though. Mine was always resembled dark water, usually with lumps.

Headlights shone in the window, and I hurried to the door. I had it open before she even reached the steps, and I stepped outside, pulling her into the warm house and my arms. We both sighed as our bodies met. I nuzzled the top of her head and then lifted her chin so I could kiss her.

It had been too long since her lips were against mine.

The bags she was holding fell to the floor, and she tugged herself against me. Groaning, I covered her lips with mine possessively. I cupped the back of her head, holding her close to my mouth, my tongue swirling and caressing, welcoming her home. She felt so right against me.

"Hi," I murmured against her lips. "How was your day?"

"It was fine," she responded breathlessly. "Although I'm hoping, not as good as my night."

I liked that.

I pulled her farther into the house, smiling at her reaction to the small tree I had bought.

"You can, ah, plant it later," I explained.

"Why are there gifts under the tree, Evan?"

"Oh, um…some fat guy in a red suit was here. I couldn't stop him."

She laughed as she bent down and added a couple of parcels to the small pile. "Funny. He dropped by the diner and left these."

"Wow, he gets around."

She stood, and I wrapped my arm around her waist. Christmas music played quietly in the background. The lights glowed in the dark —they reflected on the bows and shiny paper packages tucked beneath the tree. The candles flickered and danced, their shadows playing on the walls. It was peaceful and perfect.

Holly sighed, pressing herself back against me. "Thank you."

I kissed her head. "You're welcome."

Holly sat back, smiling at me. The house she lived in had no dining room, so we ate side by side at the counter, our hands often touching, the occasional kiss shared as we ate our dinner together. Holly could, indeed, make gravy, and she patiently walked me through the steps as she mixed and seasoned, tasting until it was right. I doubted I would ever be as proficient as she was, but I let her think I had it down pat.

"That was amazing."

"Your gravy made it work. We're a good team."

She leaned forward, nuzzling my lips. "We are. It was a wonderful Christmas dinner. Thank you."

A realization hit me.

This time, this simple dinner, was how I would remember this

Christmas. Not seeing my family. Not the disappointment I feared would happen with trying and failing to fit in with people who never seemed to want me.

No, I would remember Holly. Her warmth. Her acceptance.

Melancholy filled me, and I stood, needing to move. I grabbed our plates, walking over to the sink. A minute later, Holly joined me, wrapping her arms around me from behind. Her warmth soothed me, and I covered her hand that was resting on my chest. We were both silent for a moment, both of us feeling something in the air around us.

"Want to take a walk and see the lights before we have dessert and watch a movie?" she asked tenderly.

I turned and pulled her into my arms. "Yes."

A rm in arm, we strolled the streets, looking at the lights, stopping often to comment on a pretty house or chuckling over some badly done efforts. The night was dark, the moon full, and the stars in the clear sky bright and twinkling over us as we walked, often passing other couples and families out doing the same thing. The air was cold, but not as cold as it had been. Still, though, it was a good excuse to keep Holly close to my side.

At one point, we stopped at a house that was brightly lit, with a variety of decorations and displays out front. There was a large tree in the window, ablaze with colorful lights, and you could see the family inside—Mom, Dad, and two small children running around the room. We watched as, with help, they hung up their stockings before their parents lifted them, laughing, and carried them down the hall, no doubt to tuck them in for the night. I felt my throat tighten at the overwhelming feeling of sudden longing. Glancing down, I saw the expression on Holly's face. The vulnerable sadness I saw made me wince, and I knew she was feeling the same thing. Wanting something you thought you would never have.

"You want that, Holly? A house...kids?"

She sighed, a shaky, low sound of sadness. "I don't know how to be...*that*," she whispered, her hand indicating the now-empty window.

"Why?"

"I've never settled anywhere. My entire life has been one town after another. I only stayed here because I was so tired of moving. But even now, I know I'm not going to stay. I'll go to school and then somewhere else—" Her voice quavered. "I don't ever want to subject a child to that. Especially my own. It's just too hard. You never feel...safe."

I shook my head. She would be an amazing mother and partner. Her caring and warmth made her a natural. She couldn't see it, because she didn't see herself clearly.

I squeezed her against my side. "I think you're wrong. I think you're going to find your place. And you'll flourish. You have too much love in you not to."

She looked back at the window and sighed.

Pulling her close, I pressed a kiss to her crown. There was nothing else I could say.

6

EVAN

The movie was almost over. Holly was curled into me, the room dark except for the lights of our little tree and the dull glow from the TV. My arm was around her, my fingers caressing her shoulder as we chuckled over Chevy Chase's ridiculous antics. We had already watched *A Christmas Carol* and decided we needed something a little more upbeat for the second movie. She had been quiet for the last few moments and looking down, I saw her eyes were shut, her breathing deep and even. She was so tired. She didn't get much sleep last night because of me, and then she worked again today. Smiling, I shut off the TV and carefully lifted her into my arms, carrying her down the hall and laying her on the bed. She stirred, her eyes blinking open, and she gazed up at me sleepily. "Hi."

I nuzzled her head. "It's late. Go to sleep."

She held out her arms. "Stay."

I shut off the light and slipped in beside her after I pulled off my clothes. Wrapping my arms around her, I sighed. There was nowhere else I wanted to be.

Part of me, though, wished she were asking for forever.

The first thing I saw the next morning were Holly's blue eyes staring at me, wide and excited. Between us was a fuzzy stocking that she pushed toward me.

Grinning, I pulled myself upright. "For me?"

She nodded.

"I've never had a stocking before."

"Ever?"

I shook my head. "No. Lots of gifts, but never stockings." I looked at her sadly. "I didn't think to make you one."

She smiled. "I got one once. It was my favorite Christmas. I-I just wanted to make you one." She pushed it toward me. "Open it!"

It was full. Chocolate, socks, small puzzles, candy, and other items came out as I delved into it. Each one made me smile. Each item earned her a kiss. When it was empty, I pulled her onto my lap and showed her my own version of a full Christmas sock. I couldn't get enough of her mouth or her warmth. Joining with her was perfection. I groaned my orgasm into her neck, while she cried out her pleasure loudly.

Laughing and sated, we sipped coffee and ate toasted bagels sitting at the counter, then grabbed more coffee and entered the living room. Holly tried to hide her delight, but her eyes were dancing when we sat down by the tree. I loved seeing the expression of excitement on her face, knowing I had helped put it there. I handed her a gift, watching with barely suppressed enjoyment as she opened it. She took her time, relishing the process of unwrapping the gift slowly. Her smile of delight at the deep blue cashmere scarf and mittens was heartwarming. Her kiss warmed other parts of me.

She sighed in pleasure at the bath products Leslie helped me pick out, assuring me they were Holly's favorite scent. Holly immediately pulled out the hand lotion, insisting on testing it out not only on herself but me as well. I teased her, telling her it smelled far better on her.

I swallowed nervously handing her the last gift. The one I really wanted to give her and hoped she would accept.

She took it, eyeing the small, narrow box warily. She opened it with great care.

"Evan!" she gasped.

Smiling, I lifted the delicate handmade aquamarine necklace from the box. The color of the stone reminded me of her eyes, and I wanted to see her wear it. Surrounded by pearls, the gem was lovely and unique—just like she was. It looked perfect, nestled on her collarbone.

"It's so beautiful." Her kiss was warm and lingering. "I'll wear it every day." Another kiss followed. Her voice dropped, tinged with sadness. "I'll think of you when I wear it."

Before I could respond, she pushed a box into my hands. It was a large package, and I was filled with curiosity. I took my time opening the box and paused as I saw the contents. I ran my fingers over the smooth finish of the beautifully carved set of angel wings nestled in the tissue paper. I had seen and admired them in Leslie's store the day before. I had even chatted for a short time with the old man who had carved them, watching as he worked on another piece in the corner of the shop where he did his carving. I enjoyed wood carving, but my figures were nowhere near the delicate beauty of his. I had held these up and thought how great they would look over my fireplace, but then put them down, distracted by a question sent my way. Holly must have seen me look at them and gone back to get them for me. I remembered her casual remark of having errands to run in the afternoon. I could take them with me, and the memory of what they represented would stay with me always.

My Angel. Holly.

I smiled at her. "They're exquisite."

She returned my smile sweetly, but it didn't reach her eyes. "I saw you looking at them yesterday," she confirmed. "I thought maybe they would help you remember this Christmas."

My breath caught. I pulled her face close to mine. "I'll never forget this Christmas. I'll never forget you, Angel." My mouth covered hers, parting her lips and kissing her with all the emotion I was feeling. She returned my kiss with the same intense emotion. I pulled her closer so she was straddling my lap. She tugged on my hair as she whimpered softly. When we pulled back, I felt the loss of her warmth.

"There's one more," she whispered as she reached under the tree and handed me a long, heavier package. I leaned back, unwrapped the box and frowned. "Holly, it's too much."

"No," she insisted. "I heard you talking to Lionel about carving, and when I went back, he told me to tell you to get these chisels. He says they're the best. I asked him where to purchase them and he had an extra set, so I bought them off him."

"Holly—"

"Please accept them," she begged. "It means a lot to me. I could hear how much you enjoyed doing this while you spoke to Lionel, and I wanted to give you something useful for your hobby." Her smile was shaky. "Maybe you could make me something."

My gaze flew to hers.

"Mail it to me," she murmured.

I set aside the box. I had her in my arms again, lifting her, kissing her as I carried her down the hall, already feeling the pain of leaving her.

The morning was going too fast.

And there was nothing I could do to stop it.

She was so right in my arms. We fit together perfectly, and I wanted to lose myself in her forever. My mouth and hands memorized her taste, the feel of her silky skin. Her breathy, longing whisper of my name would forever be etched into my memory.

Being buried inside her heat was ecstasy. My mouth never left hers as I rocked, taking my time and loving her thoroughly. Her name fell like a prayer as I whispered it against her softness, my orgasm washing over me like a warm tidal wave, cresting and leaving me boneless.

I gathered her against me, holding her tight, fighting back unexpected tears. This was the last time I would make love to her.

My Angel.

How could I walk away from her?

I t was time. I sat on the edge of the bed and tied my sneakers, my stomach knotted and my throat aching with suppressed emotion.

Holly was already in the living room, waiting for me. I knew she had put my gifts in the trunk of the car while I showered.

Our separation had already begun.

With a sigh, I pulled on my coat. I didn't want to leave, but I knew the longer I stayed and drew out our goodbye, the harder it would be for both of us.

I hadn't planned on this.

My trip to see my family had taken an unexpected detour, and now I wasn't sure I wanted to get back on the road I had started on only a few days earlier. It didn't feel right.

But Holly was correct. I had to go see my family, finish what I started. Once that was done, regardless of the results, I had a life waiting for me. She was still looking for hers. We had two separate paths.

It was time to leave.

I walked soundlessly into the living room. Holly was standing at the window, her back to me, her posture rigid.

"The weather forecast is good. No snow," she said, her voice sounding thick.

I stood behind her, my own throat aching. "Holly—"

"Don't. Thank you...for everything. You made this lonely time of year so unexpectedly wonderful for me."

I turned her around, slipping my fingers under her chin. "You did the same for me, Angel."

Our eyes locked. Her warmth and caring shone through the dampness I saw there. I pulled her into my arms, wanting her closeness. We stood silent and wrapped around each other. I didn't want to move.

I didn't want to leave.

"You have to go," she murmured.

I tightened my arms.

"Go see your family. Show them how wonderful you are."

I shook my head. "I doubt that is going to happen at this point. I'm hoping for a civil visit at best."

Her eyes were intense as she tilted up her head and met my gaze. "Try, Evan. You're so special. Show your family the person you are. Let them see how special. If they can't, it's their loss. But at least you tried. Then you can go back to your life and move on. But try."

"Holly, I—"

"May I ask a favor?" she interrupted me. I realized she wanted to send me off with a smile. I knew she didn't want me to say or do anything that would make my leaving more difficult on either of us. So, I smiled and nodded at her, masking my sadness.

"Anything."

"Will you call or text me—just let me know you got there?"

I pulled her closer. "Yes."

"Evan—"

I kissed her. Long, slow, deep. I wanted her taste in my mouth for the long miles ahead. I wanted to smell her lovely scent on my skin. I wanted to burn the memory of her eyes and the way they looked at me into my brain forever. Nobody ever looked at me the way Holly did. I doubted anyone ever would again.

When we broke apart, the air was heavy. Her eyes glistened under the lights, and I felt a tear run down my cheek.

How could I feel so deeply for someone I had only just met? Why was she so insistent that I had to leave? I could stay and forget about my family. We could talk about us instead, maybe figure out a way of seeing each other again. Thoughts and ideas swirled in my mind, but before I could say them out loud, Holly stepped back, breaking the silence.

"You have to go."

I reached out and dragged her back to me. I held her close, kissing the top of her head, unable to speak. Finally, she pulled back. "Text me," she ordered.

I smiled despite the sadness I was feeling. Ms. Bossy was back.

My voice trembled as I spoke. "Holly—"

She shook her head, her voice firm. "Be happy, Evan."

She wanted me to leave. I had no choice.

I touched her one last time. One last kiss. One last glance. "You as well, Angel."

I couldn't look back as I shut the door behind me.

7

EVAN

I pulled up in front of my parents' house. It was decorated with an understated elegance that spoke of money and class. And of being done by a company for hire. It was all about appearance, not for the love of the season. I couldn't even begin to imagine my father on a stepladder hanging lights, or my mother helping him.

When one was a Brooks, one simply didn't do manual labor. You hired that out.

No wonder they were disappointed in me.

I *was* the manual labor.

I shook my head, trying to clear the melancholy that had settled in my body since leaving Holly. She had been right—I needed to come and see my family and explore the chance of having a relationship with them—any of them. Given the fact that my sister now had a child, perhaps she would be more open to staying in touch. Maybe she would be happy to see me, and we could forge some sort of bond.

I ignored the small voice in my head that informed me perhaps pigs would fly tomorrow.

I stepped from my car, grabbed the bag of gifts from the trunk, straightened my shoulders, and approached the front door. I rang the bell and waited. I wasn't sure who was more shocked when the door opened—my mother seeing me standing on the doorstep, or me seeing her answer the door. She had people who did that for her.

Her greeting, however, didn't disappoint.

"Evan," she said with a frown. "What are you doing here? We weren't expecting you."

I forced a smile. "Merry Christmas, Mother. Surprise!"

Her eyebrows rose in annoyance. There was no smile, no return salutation, and no hug.

She stepped back. "Well, you may as well come in. I don't want to let too much cold air inside."

I tamped down my disappointment. The house might be warmer inside, but the atmosphere was as frosty as the winter weather I left behind as the door shut.

"**W**hat do you mean, you don't have a dinner jacket?" My mother's voice was shocked and appalled. I noticed her facial expression didn't change a lot, leading me to think some Botox was working overtime under her skin.

I shifted in my chair, uncomfortable and tense.

"As I said before, my lifestyle doesn't require a lot of dressing up, Mother."

"You don't own a *suit?*" Her voice rose at the end of the sentence as if not owning a suit should be a crime.

"Yes, I do. But as I said earlier, this was a last-minute decision, and I didn't think to pack it. I was simply trying to get here to spend the holidays with you. A suit never crossed my mind."

She sniffed. "Showing up on Christmas Day is leaving it rather late. You could have planned better, Evan. You always were bad at time management."

I counted to ten. "I told you I experienced car trouble."

Kelsey glanced toward the window. "What year is that Buick? Maybe you need a newer, better car." Her voice dripped with sarcasm. "Surely you can afford one."

I held back my sigh. My surprise appearance had been greeted with nothing but annoyance and barely concealed contempt. As I suspected, my gifts were opened then discarded. They had disappeared at some point, and I had no idea where they went. Although I'd expected it, I was stunned at the level of indifference to the items I had chosen for them. Holly, I knew, would be devastated if she saw how they had been received.

My hopes that my sister had tempered with motherhood dissolved quickly. My niece, Mia, was looked after by a nanny, and, after some staged photos of the family by the tree, had been whisked away to another part of the house. I was allowed to hold her, but only briefly. I sat with her cradled in my arms, admiring her sweetness, and talking softly to her before she was taken away. There was no doubt they didn't want her odd uncle to have much contact with her.

"My car is two years old, Kelsey. I don't need to replace it yet. I rarely drive it since I use my work SUV most days. I need a bigger vehicle for transporting furniture."

She and my mother made a face at my statement. I wasn't sure if it was the thought of me driving a work SUV or the work I did. Neither would meet their standards.

"You will have to wear one of your father's jackets for dinner," my mother announced and stood. "Now I have to go see about the seating arrangements. Your presence makes the table an odd number, Evan. It is most inconvenient."

She walked from the room, shaking her head and muttering under her breath. Kelsey met my gaze with a cool glance and followed.

I let my head fall forward.

An inconvenience. That was all I was to them. Other than his terse greeting, my father had ignored me except to remind me once more that my life was wasted. My brother sat in the corner, a drink in hand every moment, watching the entire debacle with a smirk on his face. I wondered if anyone else noticed the amount of alcohol he was imbibing. Surprisingly, my brother-in-law, Simon, seemed like a decent sort of guy, but Kelsey interrupted him every time we began to talk. He kept trying, but when she became irate, he gave up and, with a resigned look, left the room. I didn't see him again until dinner, and we sat at opposite ends of the table. I did wonder briefly what a nice guy like him was doing married to Kelsey, but it was a question I knew I would never have an answer for. He, at least, seemed to care for his daughter. Aside from me, he was the only one who held her and appeared upset when she was removed from the room. I had a feeling there was a story there.

My brother and father had disappeared into my father's study as soon as the gifts were done. I was not invited to join them. I had sat, as an observer only, watching them open their presents, noting with interest Simon didn't participate. There had been nothing for me, of course, since I wasn't expected, and I was ignored as they opened their over-the-top gifts, exclaiming over cruise tickets, custom-made suits, expensive liquor, and jewelry none of them needed, but wanted to have—simply for show. I tried not to feel slighted thinking of the fact that all I received at Christmas every year, this one included, was a card—not even personally signed.

I rubbed a hand over my weary eyes.

This had been a mistake of epic proportions.

I stood and climbed the steps to the guest room I had been given, albeit grudgingly. I needed a nap and a shower. In my room, I checked my phone. I had texted Holly and let her know I'd arrived, and I had hoped to hear from her. There was only one line waiting for me.

Glad you're safe. Remember what I said, Evan. Show them who you are.

I shook my head. They didn't want to know me, and they couldn't care less about the person I was. I would never fit into their world and mine made them uncomfortable.

I lay down, sadness engulfing me. The wish that I was beside Holly tugged at my chest. The thought of her filled me with a longing I had never experienced. I never should have left her.

D inner was an awkward event as I sat in my borrowed jacket, listening to the talk that swirled around me in a roomful of strangers. I was rarely included in the conversation, so I spent the time instead thinking of the vast difference in the dinner with my family and their friends, compared to the one I'd shared with Holly the night before in her tiny kitchen. That small room had been filled with warmth and laughter. My parents' large, opulent room, lit with candles and heavy with the overpowering stench of hothouse flowers, was as cold and fake as the people in it. There I was, nothing more than the son who was constantly lacking, but whose presence had to be tolerated. Last night, I had been the center of Holly's small world.

I far preferred that role.

But I kept my promise to Holly and myself. I attempted to break through to them, but I failed. The following day was fraught with tension, and no matter how innocently a conversation started, it became hostile and turned into an argument. Finally, my father and I exchanged heated words over my choices in life, and for the first time ever, I stood up to him. I used Holly's words when I informed him it was my life—not his. I was happy, enjoyed my work, and my quiet life. He made sure I understood exactly how he felt and what an utter failure I was in his eyes.

After they had settled for the night, I grabbed my things and left, going through the kitchen to the back where they had asked me to park my car. Something bright caught my eye, and I was horrified to find the bag of gifts I had brought beside the garbage can. The symbolism wasn't lost on me. My gifts were worth nothing to them. Nor was I. I took them with me, knowing there were many people who would appreciate them back home.

Because Nova Scotia was my home now—not here. It never really had been.

I felt only relief as I left the house, and I knew they would feel the same way when they woke and found me gone. I no longer had to try or to spare them another thought. The only sadness I felt was at the fact that Mia would be brought up among such cold people. I feared she would become like them, and it bothered me, not that I could do anything to prevent it. I knew she wouldn't be allowed any contact with me. Silently, I wished her much luck, determined if she ever reached out, to be there for her.

I drove straight home without a break. It took everything in me not to pull off the highway as I passed the exit to the town where Holly lived. I had to wrap my hands tightly around the steering wheel and not look in the rearview mirror. I fought down the swell of desperate need to go to her.

Holly hadn't asked me to stay, so I didn't think she would want me showing back up a couple of days later on her doorstep, wanting to share my sad story. I didn't think I could handle more rejection—especially not from her. I needed to accept that she was right—my time with her had been a moment in my life. Not the future.

Somehow, that reality was far harder to handle than the disastrous finality with my family.

Holly was constantly on my mind, lingering on the edge of my thoughts. I compared everything that happened with my parents to her. Her warmth versus their coldness. Her giving, generous nature against their judgmental, rigid views. Her sweet acceptance. Their complete rejection.

With a weary sigh, I pulled into the driveway leading to my house. Lights beckoned to me, their warm glow a welcome sight after the long drive. Dan's car was parked in front of the house, and I knew he and Carol would be there waiting for me. I smiled sadly. Unlike my family, they would be happy to see me. I opened the car door, relieved to be home. Immediately, I was enveloped in Carol's embrace, a motherly action I needed more than I realized. Surrounded by her scent—vanilla and cookies—I hugged her back and let her lead me inside my house. Coffee, sandwiches, and a warm fire waited for me.

As did their patience and understanding.

"Evan, I'm so sorry. I had hoped things would go better for you." Carol's voice was hurt-filled. Hurt I knew she was feeling for me.

I leaned my head back on the sofa, enjoying the feeling of the simple comfort that being surrounded by my own things brought me.

"Pretty much a disaster from the get-go. Maybe my car breaking down was a sign. I guess I should have listened better to what the gods were saying." I smiled, trying to lighten the atmosphere, while my mind went over what I had just shared with Dan and Carol.

I told them everything about the time with my parents, holding nothing back about their displeasure or how I was done trying to be what they wanted. Moving forward, I was living life the way I wanted —with no apologies.

"Are you okay, Evan?" Carol's voice broke through my musings.

I nodded. "I'm just tired."

"You should have stopped. That is such a long drive."

I shook my head. If I had, I would have turned around and gone to find Holly. The urge had been strong. "I wanted to get home."

"We're glad you're back." Dan smiled at me. "Carol's got a big brunch planned for you. We'll give you tomorrow to rest up and come over the next day. It'll be our own little Christmas."

"I look forward to it."

Carol leaned forward, her hands resting on her knees. "Are you going to contact her? Holly?"

"Carol," Dan chided. "Not our business."

"Hush." She turned back to me. "Well?"

Carol had been full of questions about Holly. She was fascinated by the way we met and the time I'd spent with her. I had shown her the wings Holly gave me and the wood-carving tools. Talked about the time we spent together. It had been such a relief to be able to tell someone about her. I never brought up the subject at my parents', letting them think I had traveled even later than I actually had. It would have been blasphemy to have said Holly's name there. I could only imagine the biting comments that would have followed, and I didn't want to share that memory with them, only to have it tainted.

I shrugged. "And say what, Carol? 'Hey, thanks for the interlude. I'll look you up next time'? It was, as she said, a stop in my life. Something we both needed at the time."

Carol frowned. "Bullshit, Evan. That is *bullshit*."

I gaped at her. Carol never swore.

"She didn't ask me to stay," I insisted.

"And *you* didn't ask," she stated pointedly.

I stared at her, unsure what to say.

Dan let out a bark of laughter and stood. "I think we need to leave. Don't forget brunch. Come over whenever you want that morning." He pulled Carol off the chair. "We're going now. Get some sleep, Evan."

Carol paused beside my chair. "When you're ready to talk, I'm here."

Dan tugged on her arm. "Leave him alone, for heaven's sake."

She shook her head. "Stubborn fool."

I watched them walk out, not moving from the sofa.

Was she talking about Dan or me?

8

EVAN

My dreams were filled with soft blue eyes that were warm and kind. They looked at me with so much emotion, yet every time I reached for the person attached to them, they disappeared. I woke up in the late afternoon, unrefreshed and moody. I walked around the house, unable to settle.

The quiet and solitude I always enjoyed now seemed to be mocking me. The silence echoed in the house. Over and again, my eyes strayed to the wings on the mantle. Memories of my time with her played in my head.

Holly.

Her laugh.

The way she cared for me.

The sadness and fear she tried so hard to hide.

I thought of how I felt being with her.

The incredible sensation of making love to her.

How she made me feel about myself—not weak and lost. Unwanted.

Strong. Needed.

Loved?

I shook my head. I was being ridiculous. People didn't fall in love in a day.

Yet, I couldn't deny the longing I felt for her.

I glanced at my phone and picked it up. I hadn't texted her aside from the one I'd sent after arriving at my parents'. She hadn't texted me again—nor had I expected her to. But I wanted her to know I was home in case she worried.

Holly, I am back home. Things went as badly as expected. Just thought you'd want to know.

A few moments later, my phone beeped.

I'm so sorry. You deserve so much better. You tried. I am proud of you—now make your own life and be happy for you.

Be happy.

I thought I was happy before I met her.

Now I wasn't sure.

I rubbed my eyes. I wasn't sure about anything anymore.

Watching my friends open the gifts I had chosen was a far different experience than I'd had at my parents'. Their expressions of delight were a direct contrast to the tight-lipped scorn the gifts I had given my family had drawn.

Carol's reaction to the lovely blown glass vase was effusive, and Tara squealed in delight over the earrings Holly had picked out after I tried to describe her "style" as best I could. Dan was thrilled with the prints I had selected for his office, and Andrew already had plans for a fishing trip for us to use the lures I had found.

I frowned in confusion when Carol handed me another small parcel. I had opened their thoughtful gifts already. "It has your name on it," she explained. "It was in the bag with the others."

I swallowed heavily.

Holly.

With shaky fingers, I opened the little package. Inside was a small Saint Christopher medallion. The patron saint of travelers. I unfolded the small note.

To help keep you safe. Always, H

My hand came up to rest on my chest, trying to quell the sudden ache. Holly worried about me. Even after I left, she was worried about me.

The memories hit me again. The feelings they evoked flooded my system. Holly's gaze. Her caring and warmth.

I needed that in my life.

I needed her.

As crazy as it sounded, I was in love with her.

For a moment, I was lost in my thoughts until the sound of a clearing throat made me look up. My gaze found Carol's right away. Her eyes were gentle, filled with understanding, and she nodded before I even got the words out.

"I have to go back."

She smiled. "Yes, you do."

Tara sprang to her feet. "Thank God. Let's figure this out."

"I'll leave tomorrow."

Dan shook his head. "There's a big snowstorm headed this way, Evan. It's heading across Quebec right now. You'll get trapped."

"You need to fly," Tara announced. "Tonight, before we get snowed in."

"I—"

"I'm on it," Andrew announced, heading over to the computer. He sat down, typing fast. He scanned the screen. "All the flights are booked except for the last flight out at eight. I take it all the time. There's a first-class seat left." He whistled. "It's gonna cost you."

I tossed him my credit card. "Book it. I need a car—make that an SUV—to pick up there as well. A nice one."

He chuckled. "You got it. Go home and pack. I'll get this done, and

58

Tara and I will drive you to the airport. Then you can go get your girl."

I looked at Carol. "Brunch…" I started.

She waved me off with a wide smile and tugged me in for a hug. "Forget brunch. You can bring Holly for dinner when you get back."

"What if she says no?"

She shook her head and cupped my face. "Then you know you tried. But from what you've told me, she won't. I think she's missing you as much as you are missing her." She smiled. "*This* is your chance to find your life, Evan. Grab it. *Be happy.*"

"I will."

The familiar scenery went by as I drove down the road. The diner was closed between Christmas and New Year's, the parking lot deserted and the sign dark. I hoped Holly would be home when I got there. If not, I would wait.

I was nervous, anxious, and tense. I knew Holly might say no. She might think I was crazy. But like Carol said, as with the situation with my family, I had to reach out and try. I only hoped this outcome would be better.

I had spent the afternoon wandering my house, imagining Holly there with me. I could see her sitting on the porch as the sun set, our hands entwined. Or curled up in the swing sketching. I could hear her laughter echo in the kitchen as we worked together making a meal. I wanted to see her warm gaze across the table from me. I wanted to feel her pressed up against me in my bed and wake up to her in the morning.

As crazy and fast as it sounded, I wanted to build a life with her.

She understood me, because she had lived through her own kind of neglected childhood. Her parents had dragged her around, only thinking of themselves, and never giving her the things she needed more than anything. Things she deserved.

A home.

To be safe and loved.

To belong.

She had helped me. Cared for me so lovingly—a complete stranger. She had not only opened her house to me; without realizing it, she had shown me her heart. She had shared her pain and let me share mine with her. She made me feel. The short time I spent with her had changed me now...for the better. And I didn't want to go back to being shut off anymore.

While Andrew and Tara were booking my flight, I talked to Carol. She made me understand why Holly didn't ask me to stay. It wasn't because she didn't feel the same way.

No. She felt something. I could see it in her eyes and feel the way she cared for me; I knew that.

Holly didn't think herself worthy of asking. She was sending me away to get on with my life, because she thought I had a good one. But she was wrong; something was missing. She was worried she didn't know how to settle in one place or be a partner to someone, because she'd never experienced that in her entire life. But she was wrong about that also. She needed someone to love her and to let her see how it felt to have someone put her needs and desires over their own. To show her she was worth that.

I knew what was missing for both of us.

Each other.

Now I had to convince her.

I pulled up outside her house. Her large, ugly truck was parked in the driveway. I could see the glow of a light in the window, and I sighed in relief, knowing she was in there. I sat in silence, gathering up my courage; I had no idea how she would react to seeing me.

There was only one way to find out.

HOLLY

I sat on the sofa, my legs curled under me, with Chester asleep beside me. A glass of wine sat on the table, untouched. I hadn't eaten dinner since my appetite was nonexistent.

It had been since Evan had cooked dinner for us. I had barely picked at the turkey dinner Leslie made for us on Christmas Day, and in the days that followed, I snacked on leftovers she'd sent, nibbling on a sandwich or some crackers and cheese. Nothing tempted me.

All I could think about was Evan. As soon as I received his text when he went home, I read his pain in the one line he sent me. His family had rejected him.

And he had left, not stopping to see me.

It had taken everything in me not to ask him why. I knew why.

I had been correct when I'd told him the time we had was only a moment in his life. He deserved someone who could be a partner to him. Who knew how to be part of a lasting relationship. I wasn't that person, and he knew it.

Still, I couldn't stop thinking about him.

His loving nature.

His kind personality.

His passion.

How desperately I missed him. I didn't understand it, but I did. I felt empty without him.

Chester stretched, lifting his head, and I tickled him under the chin. "Evan's little twin," I murmured, a smile pulling at my lips in memory. He did look like the feline version of Evan.

Evan was tall and lanky, but his shoulders were broad. His hair, long enough to touch his collar, was a midnight black with a white patch in the middle that gave him a rakish air. His green eyes were set under heavy brows, and when he slid on his glasses to read something, his sexiness level, which was already high, flew into the stratosphere. But he was unconscious of his appeal, which only made him more attractive. I was shocked when he first told me of his shyness and absence of a girlfriend. I was convinced the town he lived in must be lacking in women with good eyesight. How he hadn't been snatched up was insane.

The sound of a car, then hurried footsteps, made me frown. The sound of furious pounding on my door startled me. Connie wasn't due home for at least a month and I wasn't expecting anyone. Chester jumped from the sofa, running to the door. I followed, worried something had happened to Leslie and Tom needed my help. I flicked on the light and yanked open the heavy door.

To say I was shocked to find Evan standing in my doorway would be an understatement.

I met his gaze. He looked anxious and upset.

"Evan? What...what are you doing here?" I stepped forward, concerned. "Are you all right?"

He held out his hand beseechingly. "I-I have to talk to you," he begged.

I stepped back, grasping his hand and pulling him inside.

"You were home. You texted me and told me that." I stared at him in horror. "How did you get back here? You didn't drive again, did you?"

He shook my head. "I flew." He tightened his hand on mine. "I had to see you. I had to try. I have to talk to you, Holly."

I furrowed my brow in confusion but nodded. "Okay, Evan. Come in and talk."

EVAN

Once in her living room, I pulled off my coat. I stood looking at her, my eyes drinking her in. It felt like years, not days, since I had last seen her. She looked so good to me. Soft, pretty, warm. I wanted so badly to touch her, pull her into my arms and hold her, but I wasn't sure if I could.

"Holly, I—"

She moved closer, now clearly concerned. "Evan, sweetheart, what is it? Why are you here?"

Sweetheart. She called me sweetheart.

I wrapped my arms around her, thrilled when she leaned into my embrace, her face buried into my chest. I held her close, needing to feel her warmth and quiet strength.

Her voice was calm. "What did you mean you had to try? Try what? Why did you need to talk to me?"

There was a tone to her voice, one I prayed was hopeful.

"I made a mistake."

She leaned back, gazing up at me, but didn't leave my arms. "What? Going to see your family?"

"No. You were right—I had to. I'm glad I did that. It proved I was correct and I don't belong in their world. And I finally told my father off. I won't let his opinion of me rule my life anymore."

She smiled and cupped my cheek. "Good. I'm proud of you. But what mistake?"

I drew in a deep breath. "I should have come right back here."

"What do you mean?"

I released her, needing to move and let off some of my nerves. I started to pace. "I never should have left here, Holly. I never should have left you behind." I tugged on my hair. "When I left my parents', I should have come right back here and talked to you. But I didn't know how you would react. If you wanted me to come back." I clenched my hands. "You didn't ask me to stay. You let me walk away. Didn't you feel anything for me?"

Her voice quavered. "Yes, I did. I felt a lot of things."

"Then why?"

"I didn't want you to go," she admitted. "It took everything I had in me not to come after you when you left. I wanted to ask you…but I was afraid. I wasn't sure how I would handle it if you said no." Her voice became thick with emotion. "I didn't think I could be what you needed."

"You are. You are *exactly* what I need."

"Evan…"

I stopped in front of her, my entire body shaking. "I want you to come with me," I blurted out before I could change my mind.

"What?"

"Come with me, *please*."

Her brow furrowed. "Where are you going?"

"I want you to come home with me. To Nova Scotia."

She stared at me, speechless.

"Leaving you behind was one of the most painful things I've ever done, Holly. The entire drive, all I could think about was you. It's all I can think about now. How you made me feel. How empty I am without you. How empty my life will be without you in it."

Her eyes were wide with surprise. I kept talking.

"I thought I was happy before. I thought my life was settled. But it's not. *I'm not.* I've been waiting for something, and I didn't know what it was until I found you. I was meant to break down that night. I was meant to find you." I paused. "We need each other, Angel.

"You told me you wanted to find your place in this world. Stop looking." I wrapped my hands around hers. "Find your home with me." I stepped closer. "I've found mine with you." I kissed her hand softly. "You said you wanted to belong somewhere." I paused. "Belong to me."

"But..."

I shook my head. "No buts. This is real. It's right. I feel it. We'll figure out everything—together. What you want to do about school. Living together as a couple. We can do it all if we're together. I'll support whatever decisions you make about your life as long as I can share it with you."

She blinked.

"Our home can be your safe place, Holly. I can be your safe place. You can be mine."

One lone tear ran down her cheek.

I took in a deep breath. "I love you."

Her voice was incredulous. "You love me?"

I shrugged self-consciously. "I know I don't have a lot of experience with that emotion. But if loving you means wanting to be with you, to make you happy, then yes. I want to protect you, care for you, like you did for me. I want to watch you smile. Wipe your tears. Hold you at night. Wake up with you." I paused. "If wanting to do all those things and be that person for you for the rest of your life means that I love you, then yes, Holly Cole. I love you."

She stared at me, speechless. Her gaze moved between our hands and my eyes.

"A very smart person told me to be happy. You make me happy. Carol told me to hold on to whatever it was I found that made me feel this way. So, I am. It's you. It's *all* you.

"I love you, Holly. I know this with a certainty beyond comprehension. Stop being alone and searching for your place in this world. It's with me. Let's live our lives together." I smiled at her, even as a tear ran down my cheek. "I want to give you what we saw the other night. A home. One filled with lights and love. A family we created together."

"You want children?"

"With you. Yes. I want everything with you." I tightened my hands around hers. "Please, Angel, rescue me one more time. For the rest of our lives."

Her eyes filled with tears. "Evan," she breathed.

"Don't say no, please. I couldn't bear it. I know it's fast, but please, give us a chance."

"I want to," she whispered.

I pulled her into my arms, relief and joy coursing through my body. In that one instant, everything in my life shifted and settled, becoming perfectly clear. If I had her, I could do anything. Be anything. As long as she was mine, I would be okay.

"What if I can't be what you need?" she asked, searching my eyes with hers.

"You already are."

"Say it again," she pleaded, her voice vulnerable.

I looked down at her sweet face. "I love you, Holly."

Her beautiful smile lit the room. "I want and feel all those things for you as well. I-I love you too, Evan."

The power of those small words hit me. She offered them without any conditions or reservations. Only truth.

I kissed her. "Those are my favorite words in the world. I will never tire of hearing you say them."

"Then I'll say them every day."

"You'll come with me?"

"Yes."

"Now?"

She frowned, confused. "Um, I need to pack up some things and let people know."

I nodded. "Of course. I'll help. What doesn't fit in the SUV, we'll ship."

"You don't want to drive my truck?" she teased gently.

"Ah, no. We'll ship it out if you insist."

"Maybe Tom could store it."

I winked. "Or junk it." I'd happily dip into my trust fund to purchase a nice car for her. But I'd pay to ship the thing if that was what she really wanted. Anything for her if it meant she came with me.

"Don't talk smack about my truck. It's been good to me." She slapped my chest, then frowned. "Chester?"

I grinned. "My cat twin is welcome. I hope he likes road trips."

"I like road trips."

"I like you."

She blushed sweetly. "What will your friends think when you come home with me?"

"They can hardly wait to meet you. I told them all about you, and they know how I feel." I drew my fingers down her cheek. "I've been searching for you. And now that I've found you, I'm not letting go." I kissed her warmly. "They are gonna love you. I have a feeling you and Tara are going to be best friends. And Carol will spoil you." I tightened my hand in reassurance. "Life will be good for us, Holly. I promise."

Her voice was quiet. "I know."

I pulled her into my arms, nuzzling the top of her head. We stayed locked together, enjoying the moment of unexpected happiness.

Holly tilted her head back. "What now?"

"I'll go find some boxes."

She chuckled. "Everything is closed. It's almost midnight. Tomorrow, I'll call Leslie and ask if she has empty ones from the store we can have."

"How do you think she and Tom will react?"

Holly smiled. "Leslie wanted to know why I let you leave. She said she knew we belonged together when she saw us together in her store." She sighed. "I'll miss them, but they knew I was leaving soon anyway. I think they might be surprised by the news, but they'll be happy for me. She and Tom will help if we need it." She looked around. "It won't take long. There isn't much. Most of this belongs to Connie. I'll have to call and tell her."

I lifted her chin. "They're just things. Take or leave whatever you want. We'll build a *life* together, Holly. One full of love. We'll fill walls with pictures and our hearts with memories. We'll do it together." I wiped away a glistening tear from the side of her eye. "You're never going to be alone again."

"Neither are you."

Our eyes met and held. My entire future was there inside the glimmering depths of soft blue. Gently, I traced her damp cheek.

"We'll start off the new year together, Angel."

"Together."

My mouth covered hers.

I was home.

Waking up to Holly the next morning was as amazing as I thought it would be. Nestled in my arms, her head on my shoulder, she slumbered with a smile on her face. I lay still, watching her for a moment, filled with wonder that I would no longer wake up alone. My days wouldn't be permeated by the sound of silence, and my nights an endless repeat of emptiness.

Holly would be there with me.

Unable to resist, I leaned down, slipping my fingers under her chin and nuzzling her full lips. She blinked awake, her smile growing against my mouth.

"Hi," she murmured, her voice thick with sleep.

"Sorry, I had to kiss you. You were making me happy."

"By sleeping?"

I chuckled. "By sleeping beside me. I realized I get to keep you." My voice caught. "I won't be alone anymore."

She snuggled closer, running her fingers through my hair. "Never again. Neither of us will be."

Our gaze met and held, our future bright and filled with love.

I slid my hand down her back, curving it over the swell of her ass, tugging her closer. "I think we should celebrate."

She whimpered at the feel of my hard cock pressing against her softness. She lifted her leg over my hip, arching her back so I settled into her heat. "Yes, Evan. We should."

I groaned at the feel of her. "You are so perfect," I whispered.

"We're perfect together."

I rolled her over, hovering above her. I gazed down at her sweet face. Her wild hair curled around her cheeks, and her lovely eyes were filled with love as she returned my stare. I slid inside her, dropping my head to her neck at the rightness of feeling her warmth wrapped around me. I began to move, my need for her overtaking everything else.

"Yes, we are."

9

EVAN

Over coffee, we planned our day and the trip ahead. I frowned as I studied the weather. "We need to leave today to beat the storm heading this way, Holly. Either that or wait a few days."

She wrapped her hand around her mug. "All I need is a couple of hours. I have to call John and resign from the diner. I already texted Connie, and she has another friend who is going to move in next week. Leslie and Tom will be here in an hour with some boxes and tape." She shrugged. "I don't have a lot to pack."

Her voice held a strange tone, and I realized she sounded almost embarrassed. "Hey," I called softly. "I told you we'll build our own memories."

She nodded. "There are a few boxes in the garage that were my parents'. I would like to take them if that's okay. And my sketchbooks."

"Holly," I started, waiting until she met my eyes before continuing. "You can bring anything you want. I'd rent a trailer if I had to, or ship everything if you wanted to bring this whole damn house."

A smile curled her lips, and the sadness faded from her eyes. "No shipping needed."

"Are you sure you're ready to do this?" I asked, my heart in my throat. "We can stay, or I can head back and you can follow when you're ready," I offered, hating the idea of leaving her at all. "This is sudden, and I don't want to rush you."

The frantic shaking of her head made me relax. She didn't want me to go without her. "No! I want to go with you. I'm just—won't your friends think it's odd when we arrive and I have, like, two suitcases, a cat, and a few boxes? Maybe they'll think I'm after your money."

I burst out laughing and leaned over to kiss her. Then I had to kiss her again. "Silly girl. When I arrived in Nova Scotia, I had a backpack. Your things don't make you the person you are. Your heart does. I already know you, Holly. I see your soul. It matches mine, and my money has nothing to do with it." I winked. "In fact, we can split the gas money."

"Good idea," she nodded sagely. "I don't think the bank is open today, but we can stop by the ATM and—"

Another round of laughter escaped my mouth, and I swept her into my arms and kissed her until she was breathless. "Not happening. I was teasing. I'm taking you home to Nova Scotia, I'm taking care of you, and you are going to let me. Understand?"

Her cheeks flooded with color. "Fine. No need to get all handsy and bossy, Evan."

I grinned. "Why don't I show you just how handsy and bossy I can get?"

Her eyes widened, and the grip she had on my arm tightened. I dropped my gaze to her mouth and I began to lower my head, when the doorbell sounded.

"Leslie and Tom," she murmured. "Bad timing."

"Nope," I said and kissed her fast. "Let's get you packed and get on the road. We'll revisit this later."

She giggled as she slipped by and patted my ass.

"So bossy."

I followed, feeling happier and lighter than I had in years.

She did that for me.

With a frown, I cast a last look at the boxes in the back of the SUV I had rented. There were six of them, plus two suitcases. That was the entire contents of Holly's life, sitting in the back of the vehicle. Three of the boxes held things from her parents—the rest were hers. I was determined her life would no longer be so empty.

I shut the liftgate and hurried back into the house. I stopped at the kennel waiting by the door and peered in at Chester. He hadn't been overly pleased at being placed inside the carrier, but he stared back at me, calm and resolved. I poked my finger inside and chuffed his chin. "You're gonna love it there, Chester," I promised. "Lots of rooms to wander around in and places to lie in the sun."

Then I went to find Holly. She had been quiet since Leslie and Tom had left, their goodbyes filled with promises of visits and keeping in touch. I liked them both and hoped they would follow through. I wanted Holly to stay close to people who cared about her.

I found her in her bedroom, opening drawers and cupboards, making sure she had everything. A small bag sat on the bed, the mittens I gave her resting beside the bag with her coat. She already had the soft hat on her head, pulled low on one side, giving her a rakish air. The blue looked pretty against her hair and skin. I leaned against the doorway, watching her. She was pale, her teeth caught in her bottom lip, and for a moment I felt a flash of guilt.

Was I pushing her too fast?

"Holly."

She looked up, a smile appearing. "Hey."

"You almost ready?"

"I was just checking I hadn't left anything." She sighed. "Not that I had a lot to bring."

I crossed the room and grasped her elbows. I bent and kissed her forehead, my lips lingering on her skin. "We discussed this. None of it matters, Holly. What you bring or don't bring. As long as you're with me, all of this is just stuff. We'll replace what you forget, and we'll build a whole bunch of new memories."

I felt her tension ease. "I know."

"Is it too much, Angel? Do I need to slow down?" My heartbeat raced as I waited for her answer.

"No. I do tend to overthink things." She laughed, not meeting my eyes. "Since my parents never really thought things out, I sort of took over that job."

I folded her into my arms, relieved. "You have me now. We'll worry about them together."

She leaned back, her smile genuine. "Together—I like that idea."

"Ready to start our adventure?"

She leaned up on her toes and kissed me. "Ready."

I slowed down as we passed the diner. It was still closed, but John had a private family party going on inside. "Did you want to stop?"

"No. John wished me well, and to be honest, I think it was the right time. His wife has been wanting to change the hours and close at eleven, instead of being open twenty-four hours. That would mean a lot of hours being cut back, and without me he can give the other girls my shifts. It used to be really busy all the time, but since they built the bypass he doesn't get as many truckers in at night. The regulars who have come for years, but not a lot of new people."

"Makes sense." I squeezed her hand, watching the way she peered over her shoulder at the building fading into the background. I knew, no matter how happy she was to be coming with me, she was going to be sentimental about leaving. "It's sort of our place, isn't it?"

"Yes, it is. But I'm so excited about where we are going, Evan."

I winked at her. "So am I."

She was quiet as she watched the scenery pass by. I hit the highway, pleased at how empty the roads were. I picked up speed, handed her my phone, and patted her leg. "Pick some music, Holly. And the route. If there is any place you want to stop, name it."

"Really?" she asked, taking my phone, her eyes excited. She had told me about the many trips she had taken with her parents. An added piece of luggage in the back seat, relegated to observer, not really part of the event or the planning. I didn't want this trip to be like that for her.

"The storm isn't going to hit for a few days. We have time to do some exploring if you want."

She leaned over and kissed my cheek, her lips warm on my skin. "Thank you."

She scrolled through my playlists, pursing her lips. "Well, thank goodness. No rap."

I felt a smile tug on my lips. "You don't like rap, Holly?"

She shook her head. "It makes me ragey. Probably not good for a car trip."

I laughed out loud, unable to imagine her "ragey." "Probably not," I agreed. "Best stick to a different genre."

"You know what goes well with road trips?" she asked, glancing at me.

"What?" I'd give her anything.

She pointed at the sign we were passing. "Coffee and donuts."

I hit the indicator and slowed down. "Your wish is my command."

She smiled—so wide and bright, it was a wonder to witness. "I'm going to like this road trip."

That was my plan.

HOLLY

Evan slowly drove up to the house, putting the SUV in park and turning to look at me. I stared at the place, awed and excited. The huge house sat on a plot of land that was astounding in its scope. Though it was snow-covered and icy, I could still see the beauty the winter hid. Mature trees and bushes surrounded a large log home. The ocean sparkled in the background. Two stories, with a huge wraparound porch and tons of windows, the house looked as if it belonged in that spot.

I turned to Evan, who was watching me with excited eyes. "Evan, it's beautiful!"

He smiled and lifted my hand to his mouth. "Yes, it is."

Except he wasn't looking at the house—he was looking at me. I felt my cheeks grow warm, and I wondered if I would ever get used to his affection.

The drive from Ontario had been so different from the ones I used to take with my parents. It was always their trip, their adventure, and I was simply present. This time, Evan made sure I saw anything I wanted. Teasingly, he told me I was in charge of the route and the radio. We strolled around little towns, spent the night in Montreal, planned another trip for when we had more time, to Quebec City. He kept his eye on the weather, but we were lucky and stayed ahead of any storm that might have stalled our journey, although he admitted, even though he was anxious to get me to Nova Scotia, he wouldn't have minded spending more time trapped in a hotel with me.

Chester proved to be a great traveler, sleeping in his kennel, sitting on my lap, watching the scenery go by, curious but calm.

Now he was sleeping in his kennel, not at all concerned the car had stopped—a seasoned traveler.

"I can't wait to see inside," I admitted. "I'm already in love with the place."

Evan grinned, kissing my hand again. "Okay."

I slid from the SUV, stretching to relieve my tight muscles. Evan opened the back door, lifting Chester out, and stood beside me. He wrapped his free arm around my waist and pressed a kiss to my head. He drew in a deep breath and smiled.

"Welcome home, Holly."

My heart stuttered with his words, but I felt only a sense of rightness. Being with Evan felt like home, and the house in front of us was going to be my sanctuary—the same way it was for him. There was no doubt about it. I returned his smile with one of my own.

"I love you."

He beamed, hugging me tight to his side as we walked toward the door.

"Those are my favorite words, ever," he murmured.

Two hours later, I was still wandering around in a daze. The house was massive. Four bedrooms, a big kitchen that took up half of the main floor, while the other half was a living-dining area. There were windows everywhere, with views of the ocean, the woods, and the lovely open areas around the house. Evan's workshop was tucked against the backdrop of massive fir trees, and as he showed me around, he explained how he loved to have the huge barn doors open so he could hear the sound of the waves and smell the fresh air as he worked. He pointed to the loft over his work area. "I'll turn that into a studio for you. You can paint and sketch to your heart's content."

I could only kiss him in thanks.

His shop was neat and orderly, as was his house. It was comfortable and furnished with pieces he had restored, along with newer sofas and chairs. The angel wings I had given him were the only decoration above the massive fireplace that heated the entire first floor.

As I stood, gazing around, Evan slid his arms around my waist, and he pulled me back against his chest. "The place needs a woman's touch," he murmured, his lips close to my ear. "*Your* touch."

"I've never had a home to add my touch to," I admitted.

He kissed my neck. "Now you do. I've always loved this house, but this is the first time it's felt like a home to me, Holly. Because you're in it. We'll make it ours."

Ours.

I liked the sound of that.

The sound of a car approaching made me lift my head to meet Evan's gaze. He grinned, the corners of his eyes crinkling. "Carol and Dan, no doubt. She insisted on 'dropping by' with dinner for us so we didn't have to worry about cooking." He chuckled. "The truth is, she's so anxious to meet you that I'm shocked she wasn't on the porch waiting when we got here."

I felt a wave of nerves hit me and Evan tightened his grip. "I'm right here, Holly. And I swear—they're gonna love you. And you will love them. I know it."

A knock sounded on the front door. He kissed my neck. "Ready?"

I huffed out a long breath. "Ready."

10

HOLLY

Carol and Dan were warmth personified. They arrived with dinner, groceries, and lots of hugs, and they stayed for coffee. By the time they left, I understood Evan's affection for them. I loved seeing her gently admonish him about making sure he kept the house warm enough for me and the way Dan teased him about how his firewood was stacked. It was impossible to feel nervous after a few moments. They seemed to accept me for simply being me—and the fact that I was important to Evan.

Carol told me about all the charming spots in town, and we made arrangements to spend some time together.

"I'll show you all the best places to shop and introduce you around," she insisted.

"That would be lovely. I need to find a job as well. Is there a diner in town?"

"Yes, a few. They are quiet this time of year, but you never know. Once tourist season kicks in, they're always looking."

I nodded, already thinking ahead. I had enough money saved; I could be without a job for a while and still contribute. I had to discuss all that with Evan.

After Dan and Carol left, I poked around the kitchen, figuring out where things were and putting away the groceries they had so kindly brought with them.

Evan strolled in, leaning against the counter, watching me.

"Holly."

Something in his voice made me stop what I was doing and turn to him. "Evan?"

He inhaled deeply and crossed his arms over his chest. "I'm rich."

I stared at him with a frown. "Rich?"

"I have a trust fund, and my business does very well."

He had mentioned a trust fund before, but I hadn't paid much attention. Confused, I smiled. "Good."

He huffed out a breath and held out his hand, tugging me close when I slid my palm against his.

He looked down at me, pushing a curl behind my ear.

"Hear me out?" he asked, his voice serious.

I nodded.

"I told you my family lives a life I'm not comfortable with. Frivolous and greedy. I rarely touch my trust fund. In fact, it's larger now than when I got it. I've invested most of it, and I only use it for important things."

"Okay."

He tightened his arms. "*You're* important, Holly."

"I don't understand."

"I don't want you to work. I want to have you here with me. You can do whatever you like. Hang around the house with Chester. Sketch and paint. Take some online courses."

"But I have to contribute. I didn't come here to sponge off of you."

"You wouldn't be sponging." He regarded me intensely. "I want—*I need*—to look after you, Holly. *You* need that. No one has ever looked after you properly before. Put you first. *I will.* I will always put you first. Let me care for you. I want to see you sleep in, relax, putter around the house and make it ours. Read. Take baths. Make us sandwiches and have lunch with me. I want you around."

He paused. "I need it as much as you do. Settle in. Get to know Carol and Tara. Decide what you really want to do, because for the

78

first time in your life, you can take the time to do so." He leaned down and kissed my nose. "I don't want you working and tired."

The thought of not being on my feet for hours at a time was tempting. Not smelling like grease and having to face endless strangers, smiling as I filled coffee cups and carried heavy trays. The idea of being here with Evan and making a home for both of us was a lovely thought. Exploring my options for school, not having to worry if not taking that extra shift meant dipping into my savings for the heating bill.

He met my gaze, his anxious for a different reason than mine.

"Please," he whispered. "Let me."

"Only if I can help you with your business. I'm good with numbers."

His eyes crinkled in happiness. "Then you're hired. I hate doing the books."

"Okay, then."

He pressed his mouth to mine.

"Okay."

I relaxed against the porcelain tub, the steam rising from the water —a mist in the air. My gaze took in the room. Evan's en suite was larger than my whole bedroom had been in Connie's place. After an early dinner, he'd insisted I have a bath and relax.

"It's been a long trip, Angel. You must be tired."

"You're the one who did all the driving," I pointed out. As I discovered, Evan liked to be in control behind the wheel. He had looked affronted when I offered to drive, informing me that it was his job to do so and my job to enjoy the scenery. I had struggled not to laugh at his over-the-top reaction, realizing that it was his way of looking after me. And I was enjoying the sights. Having never been out East— even with the snow—the landscape was beautiful. He often pulled over so I could take a picture, and at one point, had stopped and bought me a new sketchbook and pencils in case I felt like drawing.

He made the entire trip about me, and I loved every moment of being with him.

I sighed in contentment. I had never had a bath in such a large tub until now. I used some of the bath salts Evan had given me for Christmas and the room smelled of lilacs and roses.

The door opened, and Evan came in, carrying a glass of wine and a rolled towel. He set down the wine beside me and flipped his fingers. "Head up."

I lifted my head, and he slid the towel under my neck. The softness and warmth felt good, and I grinned at him. "You heated it up."

He returned my grin and dropped a kiss to my head. "I learned that from you. You heated up the towel and warmed my feet. Just repaying the favor. I ordered a bath pillow for you online, but this will do until it comes."

I gripped his hand. "Evan—you don't have to get me a pillow. Or anything else. I'm fine."

He stared down at me, his brow furrowed. "Yes, I do, Holly. It's my job now to look after you, and you need a pillow. I want you to use the tub, enjoy it. It's sat there for three years, ignored."

"You've never had a bath?"

"No, I'm a shower kind of guy. Apparently, the wife of the couple I bought the house from loved to soak in the tub and look at the stars." He indicated the skylight above me. "Never really got into that myself." He frowned. "You need candles too. Women like candles, right? We can get some in town tomorrow."

I had to stop my laugh. He was determined to make sure I had everything he thought I should have, whether it mattered or not. There was no point in fighting him. Instead, I held out my hand.

"You could join me."

He paused, his hand on the doorknob. "In the tub?"

I chuckled. "Yes, in the tub. Lots of room. I'd scrub your back if you wanted."

He stared at me for a moment, reached over his head and pulled off his shirt, then yanked down his pants. I watched his movements, admiring the way his muscles rippled.

"Maybe I need to give this tub thing a shot."

I held out my arms, welcoming him as he lowered himself into the steaming water. He leaned back into my chest with a sigh. I wrapped my arms and legs around him, then kissed the top of his head. He relaxed, his body loosening, and we lay together, staring up at the stars overhead.

"I see why she liked this," he murmured. "But I think having you with me makes it better."

I held him tighter.

"Are you nervous, Holly?" he asked, his voice low in the room. "About being here with me? Leaving your life behind?"

"No," I replied. "It wasn't much of a life, Evan. I was waiting—searching for something." A sigh flowed through my chest. "I think I was looking for you. For the first time in my life, I feel…content. As if I'm home."

He lifted my hand from his chest and kissed it. Tilting up his head, he smiled tenderly at me. "You are home, Holly. You never have to search or be alone again. I'm right here."

I lowered my face and our lips met. They moved and molded together, a perfect fit. Evan threaded his fingers into my hair, cupping my head while our kiss deepened. The water splashed as he rolled, his chest pressing me into the sloped porcelain. Our mouths never separated, if anything, our kisses becoming deeper. Our bodies sculpted to each other, the water warm around us, the air filled with his groans, my whimpers, and our heavy breathing.

Evan sat up, taking me with him. My legs straddled his thighs, his erection trapped between us. "Holly," he moaned. "I want you right here."

I nipped at his neck, running my hands over the taut muscles of his back. "Then take me."

"We're gonna get water everywhere."

I licked his ear, sucking his lobe. His shiver made me smile. His hard cock twitched, making me shiver in return.

"I hope you have a lot of towels, then."

He lifted me as if I weighed nothing, and I slowly slid down onto his length.

"I'll add those to the list. I have a feeling we're gonna be having a lot of baths," he mumbled. "Lots of baths."

I groaned at the sensation of him buried inside me, the water surrounding us, and the steam making the room a private sanctuary. I began to move, gripping the edge of the tub.

"Good."

HOLLY

SPRINGTIME A YEAR LATER

S un scattered across the water, the late spring breeze warm on my face. I carried a tray to the porch and stood looking at the dance of the waves as they hit the shore. I loved it here. The sounds of the ocean, the smell of the fresh air, the warmth of the people—and the life I had built with Evan. I studied the waves, knowing I would probably end up back in my studio, trying to capture the endlessly changing colors of the ocean. The scope here was vast, and I never ran out of inspiration. Evan had his favorite paintings framed and hung around the house and his shop and had even given a couple to Carol and Dan. He was overly proud and boastful of my talent, but I loved him for it. I loved him for everything he was.

I couldn't help remember the day he had shown me the studio he had created for me.

"Evan!" I exclaimed, trying to take in everything in the room. I met his gaze, his green eyes dancing with excitement. He had refused to let me in his shop for over two weeks. He, Dan, and Andrew had been busy—the sounds of hammers, saws, and drills going on for days. Finally, I was allowed to see the space he created for me over his shop. A set of stairs ran up the side of the shop to a wide-open space above. The front was all windows, offering a great view of the ocean and the vista surrounding the house. Broad planks on the

floor and reclaimed wood on the walls gave it a warm feeling. A huge set of shelves, an easel, and a vast selection of watercolor paints, paper, canvases, and pencils waited for me. There was a loveseat facing the window, antique, recovered, the wood trim gleaming in the sun. I ran my hand over the arched back.

"You made this for me?"

"I did all this for you, Holly."

I flung myself in his arms and kissed him. I loved kissing Evan. He was passionate, warm, and giving. His mouth was magic against mine, and he held me as though I was the most precious thing on earth to him. He growled in pleasure, low in his throat, and sat down heavily on the loveseat, never releasing my mouth. We kissed until we were breathless, yet it wasn't enough. It was never enough with Evan. With a sigh, I rested my head in the crook of his neck.

"I'm so lucky," I murmured. "You are the greatest gift I ever got."

He chuckled, his breath stirring the curls around my forehead. "I'm the lucky one, Holly. I get you."

I tilted up my head, smiling. "We get each other."

His grip tightened. "Yeah. Perfect."

"You know what else is perfect?"

"What?"

"How we can see the world from this window and no one can see us. Very private."

He raised one eyebrow, his grin wide. "Private?"

I slid off his knee to the floor in front of him. I ran my hands up his thighs, feeling the sinewy muscles clench. "Very private."

He let his head drop to the back of the loveseat as I cupped his erection, then yanked down his pants.

"Good planning on my part," he groaned.

I lowered my head, my breath washing over his cock. "You can look at the scenery while I'm, ah, busy. It's pretty spectacular."

He grunted as my mouth closed around him. Our gazes locked, his dark and intense. "I'm already looking at the most spectacular, sexiest thing I've ever seen."

I winked, unable to speak.

It was rude to talk with your mouth full.

I grinned at the memories as I stared out over the vast horizon. I would never tire of this view.

There were times I still had to pinch myself that this was my life and Evan belonged to me. That I belonged to him. Evan Brooks was every fantasy I ever had…and every dream and wish I never spoke of.

The loneliness that had permeated my life had been banished. With Evan, I found a home and people to call my family. Light glinted off the rings on my finger, making me smile. We had been married for just over a year, exchanging our vows against the backdrop of the view I loved so much. Us, our adopted family, and the friends we had made here in this small town. I had a part-time job I loved, a husband I adored, and a life I never thought would be mine.

I touched my pocket with a smile. There was something else I never thought I would have. The sound of the shop door sliding shut made me look up, and my breath caught as I watched Evan stroll toward me.

He walked differently these days. Taller, his head held high, his broad shoulders straight. His dark hair gleamed in the sun, the white patch at the front bright. He had grown more confident—sure of himself and his place in the world. His place with me.

He climbed the steps and came directly to my side, sliding his arm around my waist. He lifted my chin with his slender fingers and kissed my mouth. Long, slow, sweet. It was his hello every single day. That, and his greeting.

He smiled against my mouth. "Hello, my beautiful wife. Miss me?"

I laughed as always. "Yes, the last hours without you have been terrible."

He kissed me again. "Cheeky. You've been with Carol all afternoon. I was lonely while the two of you were shopping up a storm."

I sat down, making sure to hide my grin. Shopping had been brief. I only bought one thing.

He sat down and picked up his glass of iced tea, sipping it and looking toward the water. "What a great day."

"In every sense."

He tilted his head, studying me. "Did you find some great bargain? A new piece of furniture you're trying to figure out where to put?" he teased.

Our home had changed a great deal since I'd arrived. Evan's once bare walls were now filled with artwork, photographs, and my paintings and sketches. There'd been many trips and memories—all captured on film, our favorites displayed on the walls. Pieces from local artists we'd picked out together. Our life's story told in frames and souvenirs that made us smile. Celebrations of moments of the love that we shared.

And I had the most special one to give him.

I slipped the small square from my pocket. "I bought you something."

He grinned eagerly, holding out his hand in anticipation. He loved presents, and I had a feeling this one might top them all. I handed him the package, smiling as he studied it.

"Too small for a sofa."

"Nope."

He pursed his lips. "Not a friend for Chester. Too square."

I laughed. "Open it."

He slid off the simple brown paper and rattan ribbon and lifted up the tiny square frame. It was simple, a creamy yellow with ducks on it. Evan frowned. "Ducks. How...whimsical. Ah, a new frame for our next adventure?"

I chuckled. "Actually, we've already had this adventure. Look closer, Evan. Look inside."

He stared at the black-and-white image which he had thought to be nothing. I knew the second he realized what he was looking at. His entire body froze, and he lifted his head, his expression one of such joy—filled with so much love and tenderness that it took my breath away.

"Holly?" he uttered. "Really? *A baby?*" He swallowed. "My baby? Our baby?"

I nodded, unable to speak.

In a moment, he was on his knees in front of me, and I was

wrapped in his embrace. He pressed kisses to my cheeks, forehead, nose, and mouth, finally dropping his head to my lap. He looked up, his large hands spread wide across my stomach.

"Are you okay? Is everything all right?"

"Yes," I assured him. "Carol took me to see the doctor today, and he did the ultrasound. He said everything looked fine. Our baby is due at the start of January."

"I missed the ultrasound?"

"You can come to the next one."

"To all of them," he insisted. "I'll be there for everything."

"Okay."

"Say it, Holly. Tell me."

"You're going to be a daddy, Evan."

"I think I just found another set of favorite words."

I laughed. "I knew you'd like them."

His smile was wide. "*A baby*. Oh God, Holly, I love you."

I cupped his face. "I love you. We both love you."

His happiness couldn't be contained. He wrapped me in his arms, holding me safe and secure. "I love you, Holly. Thank you, my Angel."

EVAN

CHRISTMAS EVE DAY

Holly was asleep on the sofa, curled up under the blanket I had draped over her. I loved watching her sleep. She always smiled and muttered, lost in a dream world I would never know about. Except the fact that she often said my name, which made me smile; I liked knowing I was in there somewhere.

Today, however, she grimaced more than smiled, and her feet moved restlessly. The storm was making her nervous and disturbing her sleep. I leaned up from my place on the floor, where I had been gazing at the lights on our Christmas tree, and rubbed her rounded tummy soothingly, murmuring nonsensical words to our daughter. That did the trick, as it always did. The rapid movements stopped for both of them, and my girls relaxed. Smiling, I left my hand on Holly's stomach as I watched her, thinking about the last two years.

The happiest two years of my life.

Holly was everything I had been looking for but never knew I needed. She filled a void in my life I hadn't even known existed. She showed me how to be happy being Evan, and I showed her how it felt to be someone's priority. Everything I did, every decision was made with her happiness in mind.

Together, we built a home and a life.

Together, we were strong.

As I expected, Carol, Dan, Tara, and Andrew loved her. Carol took her under her wing, and Holly blossomed. I stopped trying to gain the approval of my family and instead basked in the unconditional love of the Whittaker clan. They became the family both Holly and I never had.

Holly decided not to go to school and instead worked as an aide in the local kindergarten. She was loved by the kids and teachers alike, and she enjoyed the freedom of not having to worry about money anymore. My favorite days were when she hung out with me in my shop, handing me tools, singing along with the radio, as I'd discovered she loved to do on our winter drive here, or chatting about plans we had. Other times she painted or sketched in the studio above my shop, and I could hear her humming and moving around, content to have her nearby. We traveled and explored the Maritimes, falling more in love with the East Coast with every new discovery.

My Angel blossomed with the love that now surrounded her. I blossomed because of hers.

So many memories stirred as I watched my wife slumber.

The day I stumbled alone and frozen into Holly's life.

The day she said she loved me and I knew my heart would never again feel so cold.

Our quiet, beautiful wedding in our home, where we promised each other we'd never be alone again.

The poignant moment she told me I was going to be a father and the joy that I felt tear through my entire being.

All the laughter and tears we had shared. The deep peace and happiness she brought to my life.

One memory stirred, making my smile even wider.

I'd arranged an overnight trip for Holly, Carol, and Tara to a spa retreat I had heard a lot about. They had a special package that catered to mothers-to-be. Holly had been having difficulty sleeping—experiencing leg cramps, and struggling to get comfortable at times, so I sent all my girls off to be pampered, hoping some massages and relaxation would help.

As soon as the car was out of sight, Dan and Andrew showed up, and we got to work. We worked on the nursery, turning the room beside Holly's and mine into a woodland playroom for the baby. I had taken one of Holly's paintings of the woods around the house and had it turned into a mural for the wall. She had added some whimsical forest creatures into her painting, planning on hanging it in the nursery, and now the scene graced the wall behind the crib. A cute bunny, an inquisitive fawn, a pair of turtle doves perched on a branch, and even a sleepy owl could be found. We painted the walls a creamy yellow and moved in the furniture I had been working on secretly. A beautiful crib and dresser that had belonged to Carol and Dan now shone new and fresh under the lights. I had stripped and refinished them in natural tones, and Dan helped me build a changing table that matched. I added a thick rug, some stuffed animals, and a rocker Holly loved from my shop. Carol had been in on the project and had sewn the curtains and pretty bedding that went in the crib. All the room needed was our daughter.

From the day we found out it was a girl, I was beside myself in excitement. I vowed I would love and protect her with everything in me. She would never doubt how much she was loved, and she would always be safe and cared for in a stable, warm home. The loneliness Holly and I had each experienced in our childhoods would not be repeated. Not by my children.

Holly's reaction to the room was nothing short of effusive. She had stood in the middle of the room, slowly turning, taking it all in. Then she'd burst into tears and flung herself into my arms.

"Happy tears?" I asked. It was hard to tell these days. She cried about a lot of things, and I was never completely sure if I needed to kick someone's ass or simply hold her.

"It-it's beautiful! All we need is our girl."

I slid my hand over her rounded tummy. "Soon," I crooned. "A few more months."

In fact, the truth was that I was as impatient as Holly for our girl to arrive. I could hardly wait to meet her, hold her, and begin to show her the love I felt for her.

And soon, she would be here.

Suddenly, I needed to be closer to Holly. I needed to touch her. I moved up and tenderly traced her cheek with my mouth, her supple skin warm under my lips. Her eyes fluttered open, and she grinned at me. "Hey."

"Hi," I whispered.

"You okay, sweetheart?"

I nodded. "I just needed to kiss you."

"Well, then—" She smiled sleepily. "Kiss away."

I pressed my lips to hers happily, and we moved together effortlessly, our kiss indulgent and loving. I cupped her face, stroking her skin in gentle circles with my thumbs.

Holly abruptly stiffened and pulled away.

"What's wrong?"

Her eyes flew down to her stomach before meeting mine. "I think your daughter is ready to meet you. My-my water just broke."

I was on my feet in a second.

"*Now*? She's early and it's storming! Tell her to wait!"

Holly began to chuckle. "I don't think that's gonna work, Daddy." She held out her hand, and I helped her sit up. "Call Andrew. He has the truck ready in case." She grimaced. "That damn Tara is always right. She said it would be today."

I was already on the phone. After Andrew assured me he was on the way and Tara would call Carol and Dan, I hurried back to Holly. "He's on his way."

She smiled calmly. "My bag is by the door. I need to change. Can you help, please?"

I fumbled, trying to get her dressed in our bedroom, my hands shaking with nerves. "Evan," she soothed. "Relax. Everything is fine."

I nodded as I tugged on her boots, unable to speak and not sure how she could be so calm right now.

She tilted up my face. "Hey."

I looked up into her warm but worried eyes.

"Evan, I need you right now. You've been so strong my whole pregnancy. Don't lose it now."

I swallowed, unsure how to explain my sudden panic. "What if—"

"What if, what?"

"What if I'm an awful father? I didn't have a good example growing up." Another terrible thought occurred to me. "What if she doesn't like me?"

Holly cupped my face firmly. "You are *nothing* like your father. You are going to be an amazing daddy. You'll be funny, kind, loving, and affectionate. Your daughter is going to adore you. Just like I do."

I drew in a shaky breath. "Promise?"

"Promise."

"Okay."

"I love you."

The words never failed to make me smile. "I love you, Angel."

My daughter was perfect. Tiny and wiggly, her skin a mottled pink, and her fist jammed into her little rosebud mouth. I couldn't bear to put her down for a second. Angela Carol Brooks had already stolen my heart. I didn't know it was possible for one person to feel this much love.

Holly had worked so hard to bring her into this world. Her labor had been long, but finally, after seventeen hours, my daughter had screamed her way into our life, protesting loudly at being moved from her little nest.

I looked over at Holly, who was watching us wearily, a tired smile on her face. "You need to put her in her bassinet, Evan."

"Soon," I lied.

Carol and Dan had been there the whole time Holly was in labor, refusing to leave. Tara and Andrew came and went, bringing food, coffee, and support. Once Angela was born, they had all seen her and Holly, then finally left me alone with my family. I knew they'd be back in the morning, so I was determined to take advantage of the time I had with my girls.

A nurse walked in and checked on Holly. She smiled as she shook her head at me, knowing full well I had been holding Angela since the last time she'd checked on my wife. "What a good daddy," she crooned. "Get some sleep, Mrs. Brooks. You'll need it." She paused on her way out of the room. "Merry Christmas."

I smiled at her. "It certainly is."

I looked down at my slumbering daughter. "I met your mommy two years ago. She was like an angel to me." I chuckled as I stroked Angela's downy little cheek. "We shared our first Christmas together, and I fell in love with her on that special day as well. She was an unexpected gift to me then, and now I have another one." I stood up and placed her into Holly's outstretched arms. Leaning down, I kissed them both and smiled as I took in the sight of both of my girls. My family.

"Now I have two angels."

My wife smiled at me. "Merry Christmas, Evan."

I kissed her again.

My Holly. My life. I was so blessed.

"Merry Christmas, Angel."

EPILOGUE

A FEW YEARS LATER...

I stood back, eyeing the large sideboard critically. It was a find Holly and I discovered one weekend when we were traveling around the island. The piece was in disrepair, the doors stuck shut from being exposed to the elements in an unused corner of a shed on a farmer's property. It was still beautiful despite the dirt, wear, and cracked wood, and Holly fell in love with it, insisting it would look perfect in our dining room. I had to agree with her and after making a deal with the owner, made the trip back with Dan in my truck, pulling the heavy piece from the shed and bringing it to my shop. I spent hours filling, repairing, and sanding to get it to this point. The doors now swung freely, the cracks and damage restored. The wood was smooth, the details brought back to life, and it was ready to be cleaned, stained, then taken into the house.

Holly would be so excited.

I pulled off my mask. The atmosphere around me swam with dust motes, the smell of freshly sanded wood heavy in the air. A fine layer of sawdust covered my shop, but the end result was worth the days of effort, buckets of sweat, and hours of painstaking detail.

I pulled open the barn door, letting the fresh, cold air rush in. The sun that had shone brightly earlier, glittering off the water at the front of the house, was now dimmer, clouds gathering and casting shadows on the branches of the trees that were gradually coming to life. Spring was slow to arrive this year, the colder weather still keeping us in its grip. I didn't mind too much, whereas once I'd dreaded winter—the long nights, the days of endless hours on hand when projects were few. Now I loved them. It gave me more time with my family, and Holly and I passed the time with our girls playing games, reading, listening to their stories, watching them grow. And with the snow came our favorite time of year—Christmas. The once lonely holiday now held a vastly different place in my heart. It was a time of joy, celebration, and family. The family Holly and I shared, as well as Dan, Carol, Andrew, and Tara.

Still, I was ready for the spring to arrive and looked forward to the time I could spend in the shop. I still loved "repairing broken pieces of history," as Holly phrased it, and the hours I toiled in my shop were fruitful and satisfying. Because of Holly, I finally accepted the joy my work brought me and was proud of what I did. Together, we had a great life.

Turning, I once again studied the sideboard, running my hand over the smooth surface of the wood making sure it was finished. I heard the telltale squeak of the back-porch door and a smile broke out on my face, knowing it must be lunchtime. I walked back to the open door of my shop to watch my girls come to me.

Angela hurried down the path, her long, straight, dark hair blowing behind her. Tall for her age and slender, she resembled me, except for her eyes. They were the same soft blue as Holly's, and they danced with mischief and laughter all the time.

"Daddy!" she squealed, launching herself into my arms, acting as if it had been days not hours since she'd seen me at breakfast. She loved to be with me in the shop, but on days when I was sanding or using heavy machinery, I didn't allow her in, not wanting to expose her to the dust or danger. When she was older, I had a feeling it would be harder to keep her away—she loved "working" in my shop and "helping" me. She listened with fascination as I showed her simple things like how to sand a piece of wood or add glue to mend a broken board.

Together we had built birdhouses and little projects I came up with, and I looked forward to when I could show her more. But for now, I practiced caution. At four, she was smart, stubborn, and sweet. I adored my little girl.

I set her on her feet, pressing a kiss to her forehead, brushing her hair behind her ear. "Hey, Angel-girl."

"We made a studio picnic!"

"Awesome." I grinned. Studio picnics were our favorite—all the fun of regular picnics, but in the warmth and comfort of Holly's studio, surrounded by blankets and soft cushions. My more "mature" bones thanked me at the end of the picnics, plus it was too cool to eat outside today. "Did you help Momma?"

She nodded furiously. "She said she couldn't do it without me."

"I bet she did."

I stood, my smile growing wider. Holly walked slowly, a huge basket in one hand, her other hand at her side. Our youngest daughter, Hannah, toddled beside her, her steps wonky and slow, but determined. Hannah was short, chubby, with a head of wild, curly red ringlets that bounced as she wobbled, clutching Holly's fingers to stay upright. When Hannah saw me, she stopped, letting go of Holly's hand, her eyes, the same green color as mine, lighting up. She began babbling in her high, animated voice, her hands flapping in excitement so fast she fell on her butt, still chirping in enthusiasm at seeing me. As usual, her exuberance made me laugh, and I hurried forward, lifting her from the cold ground and swinging her into the air.

"Hello, my little dumpling." I brought her close and blew a long raspberry on her cheek.

"Dadadada," she chortled, laughing and squirming, patting my face, reaching up with wet kisses and smiles.

My heart soared. Holly's love had brought such a sense of peace, acceptance, and light to my life, and my children's affection healed me totally. My past no longer mattered or held me in its dark grip. My girls' love was freely given, absolute, and complete. To them, I was the greatest man on earth and could do no wrong.

Unless I said no.

Luckily, that didn't happen very often.

I picked up Angela, holding both my daughters in my arms. I bent low and kissed my wife. "Hi."

She beamed up at me, laying her hand on my chest. "Hi, yourself. Hope you're hungry. Angela insisted you would be starving, so we had to make lots of sandwiches."

"Yep. Starving."

She winked. "Somehow I'm not surprised."

I laughed. I was always hungry these days. Holly was a great cook, and I had filled out over the years. My shoulders were wider, my chest broad, and my waist thick. Between my work, my girls, and life in general, my body had changed—growing sturdier the same way my determination and confidence had. I liked it. I felt strong and capable —a protector for my family.

Holly loved my muscles and showed her appreciation for them on a regular basis.

I liked that too.

A gust of wind blew through the trees, the branches swaying and bending deeply, dry leaves left over from fall dropping and swirling in the burst of air.

"Time to head in," I announced, looking at the deepening clouds. "We might be in the studio for a while."

"Can you light the fire, Daddy?" Angela asked. She loved the little potbelly stove I had in the corner of the studio. It threw a lot of warmth, making the room snug, even heating the shop below it. My girls loved to be warm.

"Yep."

Inside, I pulled the heavy door shut behind me after setting down Angela. She ran upstairs, Holly following her, and I carried Hannah up with me. She was nestled into my chest, her little fingers gripping my shirt the way she always did. She loved to be held and snuggled, and I knew if I let her, she would stay that way our entire lunch.

I had no problem with that. I never denied my children my affection. I knew what it was like to grow up with none—to yearn for hugs and love. Holly and I were very liberal with our love for our girls—and each other. After all these years, that hadn't changed.

Upstairs, I lit the fire, then shut the door once the flames licked at the kindling and paper, the heat beginning to build. Turning, I grinned at the sight in front of me. Hannah was waiting on the floor where I'd sat her, her chubby little legs kicking in impatience, her arms outstretched, anxious. I swooped her up with a flourish, delighting in her chuckles. She shoved a fist into her mouth, gnawing at her knuckles. She was a late starter when it came to teething, but she was making up for it fast.

Blankets were spread out in the middle of the room, Holly unpacked the lunch she brought, and Angela carried pillows from the pile in the corner, arranging them to her satisfaction. I sank to the floor beside Holly, nestling Hannah between my legs. She immediately pointed to the container of animal crackers, and I handed her one, amused by the way she grabbed it, chewing ravenously on it as if she hadn't been fed in weeks. Between teething and her appetite, she had something in her mouth constantly these days. I brushed my hand over her wild curls and pressed a kiss to her head. Her only response was a growly noise that made Holly and me chuckle. Hannah was serious when it came to meals, and she concentrated fully on the food in front of her.

"The sideboard looks beautiful," Holly commented, handing me another biscuit for Hannah.

"I'll stain it next week, then varnish it. It should be done by the end of the month." I glanced out the window as the glass rattled with the strong wind gusting outside. "Hopefully the sun will dry things out. It's gonna be heavy enough to carry without worrying about puddles."

Holly grinned, running her fingers along my bicep. "You'll manage."

Her touch made my body tighten. It always did. With a lewd wink, I leaned in and kissed her. Her full lips were soft underneath mine, and she tasted like coffee and something sweet and spicy—cinnamon.

"Did you bake today?" I asked eagerly.

Angela settled beside me, her cushions arranged to her liking. "We made pumpkin muffins, Daddy!"

"And raisin cookies," Holly added.

"My two favorites," I hummed. "Awesome."

Holly finished unpacking the food, and I held a plate as Angela picked out her choices. Hannah was easy when it came to meals—there wasn't a food we'd introduced she didn't love. Angela was far more selective. Some crackers, a piece of cheese, and a peanut butter sandwich. Meat was a no go for her, as were most vegetables, although she liked carrots. Luckily, she loved fruit and yogurt, and our pediatrician told us to relax when I expressed my worry over her limited diet.

"She's healthy and growing. She gets lots of protein with her choices. Let her find out what she likes and don't force her. Her likes will grow as she does." She patted my arm. *"You're doing good, Dad. Both of you are."*

I, like Hannah, loved everything, and I filled my plate with sandwiches, and all the extras Holly had made. I fed Hannah bits, listened to Angela's chatter, and sat next to my wife, brimming with contentment. I loved these times with my family.

The fire warmed the room. Holly's watercolors hung on the walls, and canvases were stacked neatly, ready to be used. I wasn't the only one who thought her talented, and in the busy tourist season, one local shop regularly sold out of her paintings. I was incredibly proud of her.

"Daddy, I'm going to school soon!" Angela announced.

I glanced at Holly, unsure how to respond.

School?

She smiled in understanding. "We saw Mrs. Anderson in town earlier," she explained. "Angela will be in prekindergarten in September."

I swallowed. *Prekindergarten?* Where the hell had the time gone? It was only yesterday Angela was a baby in my arms—and now school?

"Already?" I croaked.

Holly patted my arm. "Just part days, Daddy."

"We still get to keep Hannah," I insisted, tightening my arms around my baby girl.

Holly laughed, her head tilted back in amusement. "We get to *keep* them both. It's just a few hours during the day." She met my gaze, her eyes twinkling. "It's part of growing up, Evan."

Angela bounced from her spot on the blanket. "I'll get to spend time with my friends, Daddy. Carly is going too! I can teach you stuff when I get home!"

Carly was Angela's best friend, and I knew she was excited. Still, I had to force a smile. "That'll be awesome."

Angela jumped up. "Chutes and Ladders time!"

I pushed away my plate, my appetite suddenly gone. "Okay, Angel-girl. Get the board."

The wind rattled the glass again, and I looked up from where I was lying on the blanket. The sky was ominous and just as I was about to suggest we head to the house, the skies opened up and rain began to pour.

"Well, I guess we're stuck here," I mused.

"Not a bad place to be stuck," Holly responded. "Besides, the girls are down for the count."

I smirked. Hannah was a sleeping ball of warmth beside me, and Angela was sprawled across the blankets, having whooped my ass in three straight games. Hannah was too young to play, but she liked to move pieces around the board and, on occasion, attempt to eat them, so Holly had kept her busy, reading out loud to her while we played. Then both girls flaked out, full of lunch and happy.

"How is it possible to even think about school, Holly?" I asked. "Where the hell has the time gone?"

"This is really upsetting you," she murmured. "Why?"

"I'm not ready for them to grow up."

"But they are, Daddy," she protested. "School or not. Every day, they get bigger and more independent. And they are awesome little girls. Think how much more awesome they'll be once they get older."

I sighed. "As I get older, you mean."

"Well, there is that."

"They make me feel young *now*. As babies. I like how they need me," I admitted.

Holly offered me her hand, and I took it, tugging gently so she shifted closer. "They'll always need you, Evan." She smiled in understanding. "You're their nucleus, and they revolve around you. But they have to grow, and it's our job to help them." She cupped my cheek, her touch tender. "They love you more than anything or anyone in this world. They always will." She winked. "So will I."

I leaned forward and kissed her. "That goes both ways, Holly. They and I love you equally as much."

"I know. But you're *Daddy*. And they are *your* girls. That's special."

I ran my hand over Hannah's back. She huffed out a little sigh of contentment and snuggled closer. I smiled at her sweet little face.

"The house will seem empty," I mused. "Angela is always running around with Hannah trailing behind her. She's going to miss her big sister terribly." I sighed. "I'll miss her terribly."

"I'm sure there will be other, ah, *distractions* for both of you."

Something in her voice made me look up. She was smiling, biting her lip in one of her nervous tells.

"Distractions?"

She took my hand and placed it on her stomach. "Babies are *very* distracting."

My eyes widened. "Babies? Holly? Are you...?" My voice trailed off in excitement and disbelief. After Angela was born, we had a lot of trouble conceiving Hannah. Holly got pregnant after we stopped stressing about having another child. Hannah was another unexpected gift for both of us. After she was born, we didn't try not to get pregnant—but we didn't *not* try either.

Apparently, my old *bones* still worked. I felt my smile stretch across my face. Wide. Hard. Ecstatic.

"I am." She confirmed.

As carefully as I could, I shifted away from Hannah and knelt in front of Holly. "Angel—really?"

"Really."

I gathered her in my arms, holding her close. I dropped kisses to her forehead, cheeks, nose, then captured her mouth and kissed her deeply. Then a thought occurred to me. "How pregnant?"

She smiled against my mouth. "Another Christmas baby."

I laughed, dropping my head back on my shoulders in silent laughter. Angela was born on Christmas Day, Hannah on Boxing Day.

"What is it about spring with us?" I chuckled. "You're extra fertile."

"April Fools' every time."

I caressed her cheek. "So it seems." I ran my finger over her stomach, grinning when she giggled. She was always more sensitive when she was pregnant. "Are you feeling okay?"

"I'm fine. Tired, but fine."

"Have you seen the doctor?"

"Yes. Everything is good, and you'll be there for the ultrasound as usual."

"For everything."

She cupped my cheek. "I know." Her thumb brushed my skin. "Maybe we'll have a little Brooks boy this time. Would you like that?"

"I'd like him or her to be healthy and happy. Nothing else. I don't need to produce the next generation of Brooks men. My girls carry my name and my heart. That's all I need."

"I love you."

I cradled her face in my hands, her beautiful, sweet, wonderful face, and I kissed her. "Angel, love isn't a big enough word. It's not a big enough feeling for what happened to me when you came into my life. What you continue to do in my life. You make everything... *right*." I sighed. "You are the gift that just keeps giving, Holly. The best gift I ever got." I kissed her again. "Thank you for being you. My perfect Angel."

Her eyes were misty and her voice tender. "I'm hardly perfect, but I love being your Angel."

I slid beside her and wrapped her in my arms. She settled close, her head resting on my shoulder. I slid my hand to her stomach, spreading my fingers wide, knowing my child was resting under my touch. Holly laid hers over mine with a happy sigh.

I stretched out my legs, grinning when Angela grasped my foot in her sleep. Hannah slept to one side, and Holly was curled into my other side. I was touching every member of my family—safe and secure inside our little nest.

NEXT SUMMER

I lifted the baby swing and let it go carefully, the motion making my son laugh. I loved that sound. His sweet, high giggle that completed my world. I puckered my lips and crossed my eyes, making funny noises, and he squealed in glee. Laughing, I lifted him from the swing, holding him high. He kicked his feet and he gurgled in happiness as I slowly lowered, then lifted him back up a few times, and swooshed him around like a plane. My son loved that game.

I brought him to my chest and kissed his cheek, chuckling as he squeezed mine between his long fingers. For only seven months old, he was freakishly strong.

Brandon was another "throwback" to my grandfather. Hair so dark it was black clung to his head in wild curls, which he got from Holly. The rest was me. He was long, lean, with eyes of bright green, and Holly simply referred to him as my Mini-Me. He was the biggest baby I had ever seen, and Holly had a great deal of trouble birthing him. When they handed him to me, I was shocked by his size. Twenty-three inches and almost ten pounds in weight. I had no idea how she carried him to term. But she did, and on New Year's Eve, he was born —just like his sisters—in the middle of a storm. Holly joked it was tradition, and I supposed she was right.

We also decided three children were enough. I never wanted to watch Holly struggle that way again or feel the fear I did as we went through some tense moments. Holly was my world, and the thought of losing her was too much. Once she recovered and we talked, I had a vasectomy. We were so blessed, and I didn't want her taking birth control—the side effects she could experience frightened me as well.

Brandon gnawed at his hand, bringing me back to the present, and I dug a teething biscuit out of my pocket. Unlike Hannah, he was early for everything. His first tooth started coming in at five months, and he seemed to pop them nonstop.

"There you go, my boy. Let's go find Mommy and see what she's doing, okay?" He grasped the biscuit, gumming happily as I walked toward the house.

As I rounded the side, I spied Holly in the garden. Angela was at her best friend Carly's house but would be home by three. Hannah was on the porch, napping. My little dumpling loved her naps, but she never liked to be far away from Mommy, so I built a daybed and screened in the front porch so she could nap and be happy.

My footsteps carried me to Holly, who stood and brushed off her hands as we approached.

"There're my two favorite boys." She smiled and blew a raspberry on Brandon's cheek, then leaned up for a kiss. I happily obliged, capturing her face with my free hand and caressing her lips. She hadn't changed much, except to get prettier. Her hair was longer, still wild and curly, and she smiled all the time. As I suspected, she was a wonderful mother, a great partner, and loved by everyone who met her.

"Quite the harvest," I observed, indicating the basket beside her.

She nodded. "There is a pile of peppers, zucchini, and tomatoes. I thought maybe I'd jar up some of that homemade salsa you like so much. You can take some to Carol and Dan too."

"Awesome."

A car pulling into the driveway diverted my attention. It was an SUV, silver in color, with rental car plates. A man was behind the wheel, and as I watched, he shut off the engine, spoke to someone in the back, and opened his door.

I chuckled. "Another lost tourist, no doubt." It happened a lot in the summer.

Holly reached for Brandon and settled him on her hip. "Go give directions and get them unlost." She tickled Brandon's tummy. "We'll wait here."

I approached the SUV, prepared to give directions, my smile in place. But as I neared the vehicle, the man walked toward me, and something about him struck me as familiar. He was tall, with deep brown hair shot with silver. Sunglasses covered his eyes. He was dressed casually in jeans, a polo shirt, and a light jacket, but his posture was tense, his shoulders stiff. He had his hands buried in his pockets as I stopped a few feet away.

"Can I help you?"

He cleared his throat. "Hello, Evan."

I frowned at his deep baritone, its familiar tone striking a long-forgotten memory.

"I'm sorry, do I know you?"

He took off his glasses and stepped forward. Recognition hit me in the gut, and I stared at him. I had only seen him once, but I remembered him.

"It's me. Simon—Simon Fletcher."

Holy shit.

My brother-in-law.

It was my turn to clear my throat. "What are you doing here?" I asked, once I had made sure my sister wasn't in the passenger seat.

He scrubbed his face with his hand. "I realize seeing me must be a shock, but I needed to come and reach out."

"Why?"

He glanced over his shoulder. "My daughter—your niece—asked to see you."

For a moment, I was struck silent. Holly appeared at my side, Brandon still perched on her hip, chattering away in his baby voice, the sounds incoherent. She wrapped an arm around my waist in support. "Hello."

He smiled, the action causing his hazel eyes to crinkle at the corners. "Hello. You must be Holly."

"I am. And you are?"

"Kelsey's husband," I muttered.

He was fast to shake his head. "*Ex*-husband. We split up not long after I met you, Evan." He huffed out a long breath. "Look, maybe I should have called or written, but it felt to me like this was best done in person. It's a long story, but Mia wanted to meet you." He dug in his pocket and pulled out a well-loved worn little stuffed bear that I recognized. "She wanted to meet the man who gave her this."

I stared at the bear. I had never looked in the discarded bag, assuming all the gifts I had brought that Christmas were still in it. "I-I thought that had been thrown out with the rest of the gifts."

He shook his head. "I kept this and my tie."

"Your tie?" I repeated.

"It was a nice tie. I still wear it." He grinned, then became serious again. "Mia has carried that bear with her every day since. She loves every gift you have ever sent her."

Every gift? All these years?

It had been Holly's idea to try to keep some form of communication open with Mia. I thought it was a waste of time, but she had insisted, and every year, we sent Mia a gift and a card at Christmas. Simon owned his own investment company, so we sent the package to his office. He had been the only person even remotely kind to me that fateful Christmas, and I had thought he was the best chance of making sure the gifts were accepted. I had no idea until now if the gifts were received, but Holly wanted to keep sending them. Deep in my heart, I'd hoped Mia got them and knew that out there was someone who loved her, even if she couldn't know me.

I blinked. "I don't understand."

"I know. But I'd like the chance to explain. We've come a long way, and I'm hoping you'll be open to seeing her—to listening to my story."

I was on information overload. I had no idea my sister was divorced. The only information I had heard about my family was my brother had died in a drunk driving accident years ago and my father had retired not long after. Both pieces of news I had discovered via the internet. No one had reached out or let me know. I'd had no contact with anyone in my family since that disastrous trip home at Christmas years prior.

Holly squeezed my waist. "We'd love to meet her, wouldn't we, Evan?"

"Yes," I agreed, realizing how I must look. "I would love to meet her."

Simon smiled, his shoulders relaxing. He walked to the car and opened the back door, handing the bear to Mia inside. "Come on, sweet pea. Uncle Evan wants to meet you too."

Mia climbed out of the car. Small, with hair as dark as mine and eyes like her father's, she clung to his hand, looking nervous. "Hi."

Holly walked forward, smiling. She bent down and kissed Mia's cheek. "Hi, Mia. I'm Holly, Evan's wife. This is our son, Brandon."

Mia grinned, dimples appearing in both cheeks. "He's cute."

Holly winked. "We think so."

Mia looked past her toward me. My heart sped up at the look of vulnerability and uncertainty on her face.

My feet propelled me forward, and I stopped in front of her. "Last time I saw you, I held you on my knee. You were such a little thing. We shared a few moments together on Christmas."

She smiled. "My dad told me. We have a picture at our house."

"You do?" I glanced at Simon.

"I snapped it when no one was looking."

Huh. Another surprise.

"He said you came to see me that year."

"I did."

"I wanted to come and see you."

I held out my arms, smiling. "I'm glad you did."

She flung herself forward, and I caught her. She barely came past my waist and her arms didn't reach around me, but she held on tight.

I bent low and kissed her head. "Hello, Mia."

W e went inside, chaos ensuing for the next while. Hannah woke from her nap, Angela came home, and there were a lot of questions and activity until things settled somewhat and we could talk.

Holly made coffee and brought out some of her homemade cookies. The kids were in front of us, talking, playing, and eating their snacks. Angela was fascinated with Mia, staring at her cousin with instant adoration. Hannah was a little shyer but stayed close, making sure she could see Holly from her place on the carpet. Brandon slept in his carrier, not interested in much expect his full tummy and the cookie he gummed, falling asleep with it half eaten and hanging from his mouth.

"She was so excited to meet you," Simon murmured.

"I don't understand," I repeated. "All these years. Why now?"

He ran a hand over his face and studied his daughter with an indulgent smile on his face. He obviously adored her, which made me happy. When he spoke, his voice was quiet.

"I met Kelsey at a low point in my life. She was beautiful and vibrant and seemed to be what I needed. We got married far too fast." He met my eyes. "Outward appearances are often deceiving, as I learned the hard way. We had a lot of problems, and just when I was ready to throw in the towel, she announced she was pregnant." He sipped his coffee. "I wanted to try for our child, but it was no use. Your sister is a viper, Evan, and drains people. I was shocked at her behavior—your family's behavior—when you visited, and things got worse between us." He looked sheepish. "To be honest, you were a surprise to me that day. Kelsey had never even mentioned you."

At one time, those words would have wounded me, but now, they meant nothing. They had no power over me. I shrugged. "Not really a surprise."

He sighed. "We argued bitterly that day and all the days that followed. It never stopped and, finally, I realized I was wasting my life being unhappy and hurting my daughter. We separated later that year, and the custody battle was long and ugly."

"I'm surprised she wanted custody, to be honest. She didn't strike me as maternal."

He snorted. "She isn't. What she wanted was to keep the marriage going. Her business had hit a rough patch. Mine had not," he stated, his meaning clear. "She wanted my money and used our child to try to get it."

"Ah."

"Finally, we settled. It took me a few years to come to terms with everything. Single fatherhood, recovering from a disastrous marriage. Kelsey cut off all ties to our daughter. Your parents never see her. I wanted nothing to do with anyone from your family. Even you. I convinced myself all Brooks were cut from the same cloth."

I lifted my eyebrows and swallowed a mouthful of coffee. "That's fair."

"No," he mused. "But it took me a while to figure it out. My one and only focus was Mia—making sure she was okay. Adjusted and doing well. She was, *is,* the one good thing I got from my marriage." He stared out the window at the water for a moment, then continued. "Every year at Christmas, without fail, a package would arrive for Mia. I was shocked by the first one—Kelsey and I had just separated so I didn't know what to do with it. To be honest, the first couple of years, I didn't even open them, then my counselor told me I should— not to be so fast to write you off since you were obviously trying. So I gave them to her. Every year she looked forward to them—a package from her distant uncle and aunt." He smiled at Holly. "I assume you had a lot to do with those packages."

I squeezed her hand, loving her soft blush. "She did."

"Anyway, it wasn't anything we ever talked about until this spring. You were just a name on a package. A face in a picture. Then her class did a genealogy project—a family tree sort of thing—at school, and Mia started asking me questions. In general at first, then more in depth. Mostly about you. Why she had never met you. What you did. Where you lived. Then one night, she told me she wanted to meet you. She's asked for months, and finally, I agreed."

"Why didn't you get in touch? Obviously, you had my address."

He stared at Mia, winking at her and blowing her a kiss. Then he turned to me. "She's a child, Evan. Her mother doesn't even remember her birthday. Her grandparents ignore her. I had no idea how you would react. You seemed decent. Kind, genuine. But I thought that of Kelsey once." He scrubbed his face. "I am very open with my daughter. I told Mia I was worried about your reaction. She's very smart. Intuitive. She reminded me that you sent her a gift every year and that you didn't have to. She told me she was sure you would want to see her, but that if you didn't, it was okay, because everyone had a choice. She said she realized, aside from me, you were her only family and she wanted to know you. I told her I would write you, but she wanted to come. She begged me, and she never begs for anything. So, I brought her. I arranged for a few weeks off to make a trip of it, and we came here. I prayed all the way here you wouldn't reject her—that my first impression of you had been the right one."

I sat back, stunned, then glanced over at my niece. She was staring, her eyes wide. I held out my hand, and she stood, coming to my side. I pulled her into a loose hug. "Thank you for being brave and coming to see me."

"I wanted you to know I got your gifts, and I love them." She smiled. "I love you."

My throat got thick, and I glanced at Holly. This happened because of her. Because she insisted on trying, *on hoping*, I was able to meet my niece. I got the chance to get to know her.

Holly watched us with watery eyes.

I tapped Mia's nose. "I love you too, kiddo."

I turned to Simon, who regarded us with an indulgent smile. His eyes were suspiciously glassy as well, and none of us tried to hide it.

"Where are you staying?"

"I booked a hotel—"

Holly interrupted him. "No, you're staying with us."

"We can't impose."

I spoke. "You're not imposing, Simon. You're family."

He looked startled, then grinned.

"Yeah?"

I nodded. "I want the chance to know Mia. And you. We have lots of room, and you're welcome to stay."

"Daddy, please?" Mia asked. "I want to stay with Uncle E."

I chuckled at her name for me. "Stay," I urged.

He nodded. "We'd love to."

A FEW WEEKS LATER

I groaned as we shifted the heavy desk I was working on into place. I stood back, rubbing the back of my neck.

"I'm getting too old for this shit," I muttered.

Simon laughed, dusting off his hands. "I hit forty-two this year. Talk to me about old."

I chuckled.

Over the past few weeks, Simon and I had grown close. He and Mia seemed to fit into our life effortlessly. Dan and Carol were crazy for Mia and liked Simon a lot. Andrew, Simon, and I went fishing. Tara spent time with Holly and Mia and our children. We had barbeques and lunches on the beach. Went out on the boat I had bought and explored the island. The kids all played together, Mia assuming the role of eldest sister and doting on the others. My children loved her.

Simon spent a lot of time with me in the shop, and Mia stayed close to Holly, enjoying her company. Mia and I took long walks, and we talked about a lot of things. Simon was right. She was smart, sweet, and sensitive, and I adored her. I was going to miss her like crazy—so was Holly.

We were all going to miss them.

Simon leaned back against my workbench. "So, Evan, I need to talk to you."

"What's up?" I asked, concerned at his serious tone.

"Mia doesn't want to go back to Ontario."

I sighed, wiping the sweat off my brow. "She told me that, but she'll adjust again. Holidays are always hard when they come to an end."

He rubbed the back of his neck. "What if it didn't? End, I mean?"

"What are you talking about?"

He sighed, looking over my shoulder. "I love it here, to be honest. The quiet. The people. Our family." He stood straighter. "I'm thinking of moving us here."

"Holy shit—that's a major decision. What about your business?"

He shrugged. "What I do, I can do anywhere. I can set up an office here easily. From home, even. Yesterday when you and Mia were hanging together, I did some checking. I saw a house I liked. There's a great school close by, Mia could transfer. Aside from me, you and Holly are all the family she has, and she adores you and her cousins. I've never seen her so happy or settled, and I want that to continue. I think it would be good for us—a fresh start. We haven't been happy for a while, and I think the change would do us a world of good."

I didn't hesitate. "Then do it."

"I have to go back and arrange things. I was wondering how you would feel about Mia staying here with you while I did? I'd be back in a couple weeks and have to go back and forth for a bit…"

"We'd love it." I didn't have to ask Holly—I already knew her answer. She had cried last night at the thought of them leaving. She'd be ecstatic. "Have you talked to Mia?"

He smirked. "It was her idea. She said she loved it here and wanted to stay." He grinned, unashamed. "The house I looked at is only ten minutes away."

"You already put in an offer, didn't you?"

"Yep."

I clapped him on the shoulder. "This is great news. Let's go tell Holly."

Later that night, Holly curled into me, her face excited. "I can't believe they're moving here! Angela, Hannah, and Brandon will have their cousin close by. We'll get to see her whenever we want."

I cupped her cheek, stroking her face. "I know. Mia is so excited."

"How about you?"

"I'm still processing the fact that I get to have my niece in our life. And that Simon is a great guy." I lowered my head to hers and kissed her. "All because of you, Holly. Your thoughtfulness and insistence have once again brought an unexpected gift into my life. More family. Every single good memory I have—every moment of joy in my life—is because of *you*. Every second contains *you*. Thank you, my Angel." I kissed her again. "Thank you."

She blinked away the tears that were forming and smiled. "I just want you to be happy. You deserve it."

Her love shone in her eyes, and her actions always spoke volumes. She did it all quietly, never asking for anything in return. All she wanted was to be loved, and I made sure she was surrounded by it every day. My love for her was, and always would be, paramount in my life.

"You make me happy. Every damn day."

She snuggled closer. "You do the same for me."

"Good."

Her fingers trailed along my skin. "Did you notice the way Simon watched Amy at the barbeque last week?" she asked.

"Amy? Really?"

"I thought I saw a spark there. They certainly talked a lot. I wondered if maybe that factored into his decision."

I mulled it over. Amy was a friend of Holly's who worked at the school. She ran the kindergarten class, and Holly still helped out on occasion. Amy had come to the barbeque last week and I had seen her and Simon talking. I hadn't thought anything of it, but now that Holly mentioned it, I remembered he had casually asked about her after, when we were cleaning up. Perhaps Holly was right, and his interest was more personal. Amy was a lovely woman—kind, sweet, and a good friend. She might be the right sort of person Simon needed to move on.

"I guess we'll see."

She laughed quietly. "I'm going to go have coffee with her and do a little digging."

I tucked her closer. "My little matchmaker."

We were quiet as thoughts drifted through my head. I could see the years ahead. Our families blending. Watching Mia and my children growing up together. Spending more time with Simon. He had already expressed an interest in helping coach hockey with me in the winter. We had sat down and figured out the next while as he went back and forth to settle things in Ontario and make the move here. Mia was excited about staying with us and seeing more of Carol and Dan, who had taken on the role of grandparents the same way they had with my kids.

I saw it all. Birthdays, celebrations, holidays—especially Christmas. From what Simon had said, they had never had one at home. He usually took them on a trip since he couldn't face the holiday on his own. When Holly talked about how we celebrated—especially with three birthdays at the same time—Mia's eyes grew huge in her face, excitement pouring off her. She'd never seen a real white Christmas, and we always had snow. We'd have to make this year's festivities especially good. And if Simon found someone to share his life with, all the better. After what he went through, he deserved it.

As if reading my mind, Holly hummed. "You're thinking about the holidays already, aren't you?"

I chuckled. "My favorite time of year for so many reasons. It was the start of us. Of this amazing life. Who knew a broken-down car would lead me to you?"

She cupped my face. "It was fate. And we have a whole lifetime together, Evan. We're still just beginning. Every day is a new adventure."

I kissed her full lips, grateful for her and all the blessings she had brought into my life. She was right. Each day was a new adventure, and with her by my side, life promised to be filled with them.

"I know, Angel. I know. I look forward to every single one."

She sighed in happiness. "I love you," she whispered.

I smiled, pressing my lips to her head.

Those were still my favorite words.

"Love you too, Angel. Always."

ACKNOWLEDGMENTS

This is a short book, so I will keep this part short as well.

To my team— thank you.

To my readers—you humble me.

To the bloggers, and my reading group, the Minions and social media posters—you rock.

Lisa – thanks for the humor and help.

Deb and Peggy - thank you for your keen eyes and support.

Karen, my wonderful, amazing PA – I cannot do without you.
You are so vital to the book world we share,
and to me as a friend. So much love.

ALSO BY MELANIE MORELAND

Vested Interest Series

Bentley (Vested Interest #1)

Aiden (Vested Interest #2)

Maddox (Vested Interest #3)

Reid (Vested Interest #4)

Van (Vested Interest #5)

Halton (Vested Interest #6)

Insta-Spark Collection

It Started with a Kiss

Christmas Sugar

An Instant Connection

The Contract Series

The Contract (The Contract #1)

The Baby Clause (The Contract #2)

The Amendment (The Contract #3)

Standalones

Into the Storm

Beneath the Scars

Over the Fence

My Image of You (Random House/Loveswept)

ABOUT THE AUTHOR

New York Times/USA Today bestselling author Melanie Moreland, lives a happy and content life in a quiet area of Ontario with her beloved husband of thirty plus years and their rescue cat, Amber. Nothing means more to her than her friends and family, and she cherishes every moment spent with them.

While seriously addicted to coffee, and highly challenged with all things computer-related and technical, she relishes baking, cooking, and trying new recipes for people to sample. She loves to throw dinner parties, and enjoys traveling, here and abroad, but finds coming home is always the best part of any trip.

Melanie loves stories, especially paired with a good wine, and enjoys skydiving (free falling over a fleck of dust) extreme snowboarding (falling down the stairs) and piloting her own helicopter (tripping over her own feet). She's learned happily ever afters, even bumpy ones, are all in how you tell the story.

Melanie is represented by Flavia Viotti at Bookcase Literary Agency. For any questions regarding subsidiary or translation rights please contact her at flavia@bookcaseagency.com

Connect with Melanie

Like reader groups? Lots of fun and giveaways! Check it out on Facebook at Melanie Moreland's Minions!

Join my newsletter for up-to-date news, sales, book announcements and excerpts (no spam). Sign up at:

Melanie Moreland's Newsletter

My Website - www.melaniemoreland.com

Made in the USA
Middletown, DE
14 May 2020